# FREEDOM BOUND

OTHER BOOKS BY
JEAN RAE BAXTER

*Broken Trail* (2011)

*Scattered Light* (2011)

*Looking for Cardenio* (2008)

*The Way Lies North* (2007)

*A Twist of Malice* (2005)

# Freedom
# Bound

JEAN RAE BAXTER

RONSDALE PRESS

RONSDALE PRESS
3350 West 21st Avenue, Vancouver, B.C., Canada V6S 1G7
www.ronsdalepress.com

Typesetting: Julie Cochrane, in Minion 12 pt on 16
Cover Art & Design: Massive Graphic
Maps: Jean Rae Baxter and Veronica Hatch
Paper: Ancient Forest Friendly "Silva" (FSC)—100% post-consumer waste,
   totally chlorine-free and acid-free

Ronsdale Press wishes to thank the following for their support of its publishing
program: the Canada Council for the Arts, the Government of Canada through
the Canada Book Program, the British Columbia Arts Council and the Province
of British Columbia through the British Columbia Book Publishing Tax Credit
program.

**Library and Archives Canada Cataloguing in Publication**

Baxter, Jean Rae, 1932–
   Freedom bound / Jean Rae Baxter.

Issued also in an electronic format.
ISBN 978-1-55380-143-6

   1. United Empire loyalists—Juvenile fiction. 2. United States—
History—Revolution, 1775–1783—Juvenile fiction. 3. Canada—
History—1775–1783—Juvenile fiction. I. Title.

PS8603.A935F74 2012      jC813'.6      C2011-906812-5

Printed in Canada by Marquis Printing, Quebec

*for Leigh*

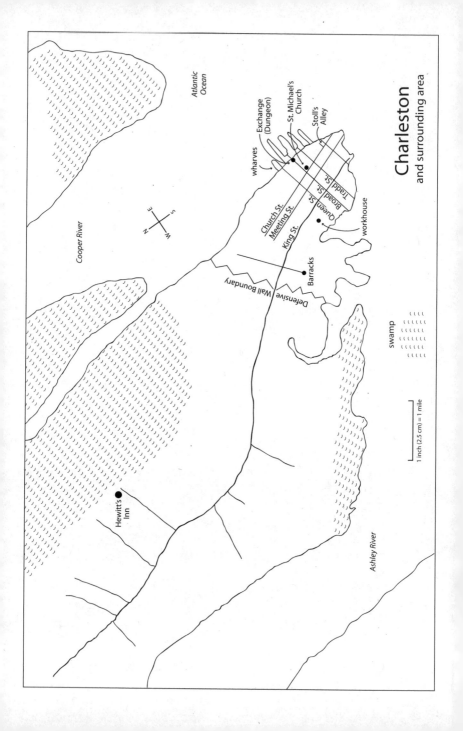

# Charleston
and surrounding area

Atlantic Ocean

Cooper River

Ashley River

Hewitt's Inn

Defensive Wall Boundary

Barracks

King St.

Meeting St.

Church St.

Queen St.

Broad St.

Tradd St.

wharves

Exchange (Dungeon)

St. Michael's Church

Stoll's Alley

workhouse

swamp

1 inch (2.5 cm) = 1 mile

# Chapter 1

## JANUARY 1781

SHE COULDN'T SEE Nick anywhere.

Charlotte stood at the bow, her eyes searching the wharves as the *Blossom* entered Charleston Harbour. Around her, the other passengers' voices mingled with the sounds of sailors shouting, water lapping against the wooden hull, spars creaking and gulls shrieking.

The harbour was clogged with ships. There were warships of King George's Royal Navy, merchant ships, transport ships, slave ships, and the hulks that held prisoners of war. Except for the hulks, every ship carried guns. Even the *Blossom*, with its twelve passengers and its cargo of tallow and hides, was armed with twenty guns. What with French, Spanish and rebel warships on the hunt for any vessel flying a British flag, the seas were perilous all the way from Nova Scotia to the Carolinas.

At Charlotte's side stood Mrs. Dickinson, the purser's wife. The only other woman on board, she was short and sturdy, with a red nose and cheeks roughened by sun and wind.

"Do you see him yet?" Mrs. Dickinson asked.

"Not yet. When we're closer, he'll be easy to spot. Nick's very tall."

But when the ship moored at its wharf and the sailors were lowering the rope ladder over the side, Charlotte still had not seen him.

"Even if I can't spot him in the crowd, he's sure to see me," said Charlotte. "I'll be the only woman climbing down the ship's ladder, except for you."

"Me! Merciful heavens! You won't catch me on that ladder one more time than I can help! Climbing it to come aboard was quite enough for me."

"Don't you want to see Charleston?"

"No, thank you." Mrs. Dickinson shook her head firmly. "From what I hear, the streets swarm with refugees, cut-purses and runaway slaves. I've no wish to go ashore. My only reason for going to sea is to be with my husband. If I didn't, I'd never see him at all."

"I know what that's like. Nick and I have been married more than a year. In all that time, we've spent a total of twenty-two days together."

"At that rate, you can hardly call yourself married, if you ask me."

"There've been times I thought so, too. But everything's about to change. After three years as a courier, Nick has been attached to the Civilian Department of the Southern Command. He's been given a room of his own in the officers' quarters, and I have come to Charleston to join him."

Charlotte stepped away from the rail. "If you'll excuse me, Mrs. Dickinson, I'm eager to go ashore."

"My best wishes go with you!"

"Goodbye and thank you. It's been a comfort not to be the only woman on the ship."

Hurrying to the spot where sailors had lowered the rope ladder, Charlotte was first in line when the gate in the rail was opened.

"Careful there, young lady!" a sailor warned, holding out his hand to offer help. But she was already over the side, her foot reaching for the next rung down.

"That lass is fit for a life at sea," another sailor laughed.

"I'd like to see her up in the rigging," the first chortled, "with those skirts blowing in the wind."

She pretended not to hear.

Charlotte was eighteen years old. She had black hair, pink cheeks, and lively brown eyes. For her arrival in Charleston, she was wearing a blue cloak over a plum-coloured woollen gown—her first new garments in four years. Nick had sent five pounds sterling from his pay so that she could purchase clothes in Quebec before embarking.

If she had been wearing breeches on the voyage and not a long cloak and gown, she would have loved to climb up in the rigging, where wind filled the sails, as far away as possible from her berth between the decks.

Charlotte thought that whoever gave the *Blossom* that name must have had an odd sense of humour, for her quarters had reeked of pitch, bilge water, and human waste—a noxious stench that nearly turned her stomach. She had heard rats skittering and squeaking, and sometimes she saw one. Although it was cold on the Atlantic in winter, she had spent almost every waking moment on deck. Even so, she felt as if the stink of the ship would cling to her clothes forever.

As soon as she was standing on the wharf, Charlotte resumed her search for Nick, her mind refusing to accept what her eyes told her.

A young officer stood a few yards away, his red coat and white cross belts making him stand out from the crowd. From under the brim of his tricorn peered a pair of eyes that seemed fixed on her. She turned away, avoiding eye contact. As she continued to look for Nick, she could not suppress the rising fear that something had gone wrong.

When she happened to notice the young officer again, he was still staring at her. The steadiness of his gaze forced the truth upon her. Nick was not here. This stranger had come to meet her. Their eyes met. She did not look away.

The young officer stepped forward. He bowed.

"Have I the honour of addressing Mrs. Charlotte Schyler?"

"I am Charlotte Schyler." She held her breath, waiting.

"Captain Ralph Braemar, South Carolina Royalist Regiment, at your service. Nick asked me to meet you. He is most unhappy not to be here."

"Has something happened to him?"

"No. Nick is well."

"Then why . . . why isn't he here to meet me?" Her words caught in her throat. She had travelled three weeks in a stinking ship, enduring every kind of hardship cheerfully because she believed that as soon as she stepped ashore, Nick would be there to welcome her.

Captain Braemar looked around before he spoke, as if to make certain that no one could overhear. "He's been ordered to the backcountry."

"You mean the army is still using him as a courier? I thought that was finished. He wrote to me that he's now attached to the Civilian Department."

"He was. But the military needed someone to go into the interior of South Carolina to gather information. We think there's considerable support for the King, but with so much persecution of Loyalists, hundreds have taken to the swamps to hide. General Cornwallis needs to know how much active support the army can expect. Nick has the skills to find that out."

Her voice shook. "Are you telling me that Nick is a spy?"

"Shh!" His voice sank to a whisper. "You could say that. But you don't need to worry. If the rebels couldn't capture him when he was a courier, they can't catch him now."

"I suppose you're right." She wanted to believe this. For

three years she had forced herself not to worry about Nick. But she knew that a spy, like a courier, faced hanging if he were captured.

"As soon as he received his orders, Nick wrote to warn you not to come to Charleston. His letter went by ship to Canada about six weeks ago. Since he knew it was unlikely to reach you in time to stop you from setting out, he made me promise to meet every ship. He didn't want you to arrive and find no one waiting."

She looked around at the dozens of wharves and the dozens of ships at dockside or anchored in the harbour.

"You've met every single ship that arrived this winter?"

"Yes, ma'am. I haven't missed one ship flying the British flag."

"Thank you, Captain Braemar. I am most grateful."

"It was no more than friendship requires." He bowed again. "Now let's find your trunk. If we stand on the steps of the Exchange, we can watch the wharfingers unload the ship. They always start with the passengers' boxes. As soon as those are on the wharf, I'll hire a man with a pushcart to carry your trunk." He offered Charlotte his arm.

"Is the Exchange that beautiful big building on the waterfront?" She took his arm. "It's so grand, I thought it must be the Governor's palace."

"No ma'am. The Exchange is our customhouse. It was built for commerce and for important social events. Underneath there's a vault where we lock up political prisoners."

"Oh." She shivered. "A dungeon?"

"Yes. We call it the Provost Dungeon. It wasn't built to be a dungeon, but that's what it's used for now. We don't have enough room in the hulks to hold all the prisoners of war, and the city jail has been turned into barracks for soldiers. Charleston is an occupied city, you know, and we're at war."

"Nick warned me that I wouldn't like everything I saw."

"It's not so bad, really. You'll be comfortable in the officers' quarters. Nick is lucky they assigned him a room."

When they had mounted the steps of the Exchange, they stood watching as the wharfingers, manning a clumsy wooden crane, unloaded an assortment of boxes and trunks and sea chests onto the dock.

"I see my trunk," she said after a few minutes.

"Wait here. I'll find a carter." He walked down the steps, leaving her waiting.

Charlotte pulled her cloak closer about her shoulders. She felt a twinge of panic as Captain Braemar disappeared in the crowd. What if something happened to him? Then what would she do in this unfamiliar city where she didn't know a soul?

# Chapter 2

CHARLOTTE'S ANXIETY SOON ended. In a couple of minutes Captain Braemar reappeared, followed by a black man with a pushcart. She walked down the steps of the Exchange to join them. "That one's mine." She pointed to a wooden trunk bound with brass straps.

Captain Braemar helped the man lift it onto his cart.

"I hope you don't mind a walk," he said to Charlotte.

"I'm happy to walk. I need to find my land legs again."

Once she started walking, she was less happy to be on foot. The street was unpaved, soft and slimy. Charlotte's first impression of Charleston was that it smelled nearly as bad as the *Blossom*.

"Do you know much about Charleston?" Captain Braemar asked.

"Very little."

"It's built on a peninsula that's shaped like a tongue. On the west side, there's the Ashley River. On the east side, there's the Cooper River. Charleston Harbour is where they join."

"Do you know the town well?"

"I should know it! I was born and raised here. My family has a house in town, where we spend part of the year. The rest of the time we live on our rice plantation, Bellevue, twenty-five miles up the Ashley."

While they talked, Captain Braemar frequently looked back over his shoulder, apparently checking to see that the carter still followed. Either he's worried lest we become separated in the crowd, Charlotte thought, or he's afraid the man may run off with my trunk.

"There is such a quantity of people," she observed. "I've never before seen so many in one place. And most of them are black."

"Before the war began, whites and blacks were more or less in equal number. But now the blacks outnumber the whites. We have about thirty-eight thousand black people to eleven thousand white."

"I suppose all the black people are slaves."

"Most are slaves, but some are free."

"How do you tell them apart?"

"A slave going about town must carry a pass that says he's

on his master's business. The man I just hired to bring your trunk is free and has a certificate to prove it." Captain Braemar looked around again. The carter was still with them.

They were passing a stately building with an open portico, two tall pillars flanking the door. Chained to one of the pillars was a black man. His back was bare, and he was being whipped. His head hung to one side, and he made no sound that Charlotte could hear, although she was near enough to hear the whoosh of the lash and the smack as it struck his skin. Blood welled from the open cuts. A dozen or so spectators—black and white—stood watching.

She stopped walking. Once, on the *Blossom*, she had seen a sailor being flogged, but not with such ferocity. The man wielding the whip had his teeth bared in a savage grin. He's enjoying this, Charlotte thought, and she shuddered.

"Come away," Captain Braemar said. "You don't want to watch this." When he tugged her arm gently, she yielded and they walked on.

"What could that poor man have done to deserve such punishment?"

"Most likely he's a runaway. One hundred lashes for correction." He spoke as if explaining something to a child, bending his head toward her to be sure she heard. "He's getting off lightly. Sometimes they tie a nail to the whip."

"It's horrible."

"Yes ma'am. It is horrible. And it's a horror we brought upon ourselves."

"You mean, slavery?"

"I'm not against slavery. The prosperity of South Carolina depends on it. We couldn't grow rice and indigo without slaves to do the work."

"You could hire people, couldn't you?"

"Costs too much. And you wouldn't find many white men who'd want to do it. No ma'am, the slave system is the only one that will work in the South. And it worked well until British policy makers hatched the idea that we could hurt the rebels by offering freedom to their slaves. All a slave had to do was stay behind British lines for one year, helping the military. At the end of the year, he'd be granted a General Birch certificate. Owning that certificate makes him a free man."

"It sounds to me like a good idea."

"Too good, as it's turned out. Word spread from one plantation to the next. Thousands of runaway slaves flocked to every town behind British lines. Most didn't know which side their owner was on. All they heard was 'Freedom.'"

"Who can blame them?"

"I can't say I do blame them. The problem is, only slaves owned by rebels qualify for a General Birch certificate. If the owner is a Loyalist, we send his slaves right back to him. That makes them angry. Many refuse to carry out their duties, or perform them poorly. So their owners must use harsh measures to keep them in line."

Charlotte glanced back over her shoulder at the man

chained to the pillar. The more he slumped, the more vigorously his tormenter wielded the whip. Was this an example of harsh measures? It made her feel sick.

He continued. "Since last May, after we took Charleston from the rebels, the situation has become worse. General Clinton, the British Commander in Chief at the time, issued a proclamation offering full restoration of property and civil rights to all rebels who would swear allegiance to King George. In Charleston alone, more than two thousand men accepted the offer. 'Now that we've returned to our allegiance,' they said, 'kindly give us back our slaves.'

"But the genie was out of the bottle. Those newly freed slaves were now serving in black regiments or working on fortifications. To return them to slavery would have been impossible. So there's plenty of bad feeling all around."

Charlotte and Captain Braemar turned onto a street that had a brick sidewalk—clearly a better part of town. The houses here were large and elegant. Along the sidewalks grew the strangest trees that she had ever seen. Instead of branches, each tree had a clump of long, bristling leaves stuck on top of a bare trunk.

"What are those trees?"

"Palmettos. I guess you've never seen them before."

"There's a lot I've never seen before." She could have added, *and I don't just mean trees.* But she didn't say it out loud.

They stopped in front of a handsome three-storey house that stood behind a wall with a wrought-iron gate. It had two verandas, an upper and a lower, that extended on one side of the house all the way from the front to the back.

"Here we are," he said. "The officers' quarters."

"Why, it's a mansion! At Fort Haldimand on Carleton Island, the officers' quarters are a wing of the barracks."

"This is Charleston, not a fort on an island in the middle of the wilderness. Here, officers are billeted in the better homes. In this case, Southern Command took over an entire house for their use."

"Is this where you live?"

"No. Since my family owns a house in Charleston, I live at home."

While Captain Braemar and the carter lifted the trunk from the cart, Charlotte gazed in awe at the magnificent dwelling in front of her. Would she really be living here? What a contrast to the army tent that had been her family's first home in the refugee camp on Carleton Island, and to the little log cabin that she and her father had built last summer! What would Papa say if he could see this mansion?

"Will you open the gate for us? Our hands are full." Captain Braemar's voice broke into her thoughts. He sounded amused, and she realized that she had been acting like a country bumpkin, staring at the house.

"Oh, sorry."

She unlatched the gate so that they could carry her trunk through, and then walked ahead of them to open the front door.

When the trunk had been set down in the entrance hall,

Captain Braemar handed the carter a coin. Touching his fingers to his forehead, the black man said, "Thank you, sir." To Charlotte, the way he pronounced it sounded like "Suh."

The room that lay before her was large. Silk curtains hung at the windows. Enormous mirrors in gilded frames adorned the panelled walls. On the marble mantelpiece gleamed silver candlesticks, the candles unlit since ample light streamed through the tall windows. There were wingback chairs by the fireplace, as well as an upholstered settee. Four officers sat at a table, playing cards.

"I'll present you to Colonel Knightly," the captain said, "and then take my leave. I wish I could stay to see you settled, but I'm due at Headquarters and must not tarry."

"Thank you for escorting me here." Charlotte straightened her shoulders and lifted her chin, trying not to appear overawed by her surroundings. "I'm sure I'll settle in with no problem."

One of the officers rose from his chair. He wore a red coat of fine wool, with buff collar, cuffs and lapel. Around his ample waist was a crimson sash, and on his head a white periwig. He was a portly gentleman, about fifty years of age.

"May I present Mrs. Charlotte Schyler," said Captain Braemar.

The colonel bowed politely, but he looked at Charlotte as if he had never heard of her, as if he did not expect her at all.

As soon as the introduction was completed, the captain departed. The three officers at the card table looked up. Their faces showed signs of impatience.

"Excuse me for interrupting your pastime," Charlotte said with as much dignity as she could muster. "I'm newly arrived from Canada. My husband has a room here in the officers' quarters. If someone will kindly show me to it—"

"My dear Mrs. Schyler, this is most awkward." She heard the embarrassment in the colonel's voice. "Recently we received a large number of reinforcements, with the result that every available room was needed."

"You mean, I can't stay here?"

"Uh . . ." He cleared his throat. "When your husband left for the backcountry, we put his possessions into storage. Captain Antrim now has the room that was assigned to him."

"Oh . . . where am I to stay?"

"That is the question. Since we have no accommodation for you here, some other arrangement will be necessary."

"I don't know anybody in Charleston. I have no friends to take me in." She felt stunned and helpless. Everything was going wrong. No Nick. No place to live.

She had travelled for two weeks in an open bateau from Carleton Island down the St. Lawrence River to Quebec City, and then been tossed about at sea for three more weeks. Charlotte was exhausted. A roaring filled her ears, and she felt the floor tilting. Darkness came over her in a rush.

# Chapter 3

SHE WOKE CHOKING, and jerked her head back and forth to escape the pungent fumes that seared her nostrils. When she opened her eyes, she saw a slender white hand holding a glass vial under her nose. Smelling salts, of course. The next moment, she realized that she was lying on the settee in front of the fire and that someone was perched beside her on the edge of the seat.

Lifting her eyes higher, she saw that the person beside her was an elegantly dressed woman.

"Awake, my dear? You gave my husband a terrible fright. He was too blunt with you, I fear. That's his way. Well, I declare, he shall do his penance now."

Charlotte gave her head a shake. A moment passed before she understood. "Is your husband the colonel?"

"Yes, he is. I am Clara Knightly. And I am so sorry for the rude welcome you received." She closed the vial and placed it in the dainty reticule that hung from her wrist. "Poor young creature! As if we would thrust you out of doors like a beggar!"

Charlotte struggled to sit up. She didn't like being called a poor young creature. "I've never fainted before," she spluttered, trying to cover her embarrassment.

"Do not fret. Every young lady is entitled to have the vapours now and then. Don't you worry about anything. The colonel has sent a man to make enquiries of a Quaker woman who may be able to give you lodging. Nick has mentioned to us that he has friends among the Quakers. As for tonight, I have told Colonel Knightly that he must sleep here in the common room, because you are going to share my bed."

"Oh, no! I would not presume."

"I insist. We shall be like sisters. Now, if you are sufficiently recovered, I'll take you upstairs. Your trunk is already there." Mrs. Knightly stood up. "My slave Posy is heating water for your bath. After bathing, you may either dine with my husband and me or sup from a tray in private. The choice is yours."

"Thank you. Then I choose the tray, for I am exceedingly tired."

This lady seemed to assume that she could take over

Charlotte's life. But for one night, why not let her? After three weeks on board the *Blossom*, the idea of a bath was irresistible. She did have to sleep somewhere. And so she decided to make no further objection.

Outside, the daylight was fading. A small black boy in blue livery moved about the room, lighting candle after candle. Soon dozens of lights were reflected in the tiny panes of window glass.

"Come along, then." Mrs. Knightly held out her hand. Her fingers were white and smooth, and on one she wore a sapphire ring. Her gown was as blue as the sapphire. It had deep flounces at the sides, each flounce trimmed with a ruffle. Her figure was graceful, her complexion perfect, and she looked twenty years younger than her husband.

Charlotte took the offered hand and stood up carefully, not sure how steady on her feet she would be, and followed her from the room.

They walked side by side up a curving staircase and along a hall, stopping in front of a gleaming mahogany door. Mrs. Knightly drew a key from her reticule, and turned it in the lock.

The door opened, revealing a high bed with red velvet hangings, a satin coverlet, and snowy white pillows piled at the head.

Charlotte gasped. Such luxury!

At the sight of those spotless pillows, she reckoned she knew the real reason why Mrs. Knightly was so keen on her taking a bath. Who would want to share a bed with a person who reeked of bilge water?

A copper hipbath stood near the hearth, where a small fire burned. Steam rose from the bath.

"Posy is likely fetching more water. She will see to your needs."

"I don't need help to take a bath."

"My slave is well trained. You won't find her attentions offensive." Mrs. Knightly took a step toward the door. "I'll give the cook directions for your supper tray. After you've eaten, no one will disturb you. If you're asleep when I return, I'll be very quiet and try not to waken you."

When Mrs. Knightly had left the room, Charlotte opened her trunk and took out the nightgown she had purchased in Quebec before embarking. It was made of fine white cotton, with lace at the bodice. She had bought this nightgown with Nick in mind, dreaming of the honeymoon that they had never had. Even though Nick was not here, she was glad she had bought it. A bed with velvet hangings and satin pillows called for something better than a worn linsey-woolsey shift.

As Charlotte was unfolding her nightgown, a black woman entered carrying a ewer from which steam rose. She was tall and graceful, with skin as black as ebony. Around her slender neck was a brass collar. It was hinged, with a lock at the back. Instinctively, Charlotte raised her fingers to her own throat, imagining how it must feel.

Silently the slave woman emptied the water into the tub. Instead of then leaving the room, she stood by, apparently expecting to help Charlotte take her bath.

Well, I don't need help taking off my clothes, she thought, so I might as well get started.

As Charlotte undressed, Posy took each garment from her. First her gown, then the belt under her gown from which her pocket hung, and then her petticoat. At first she felt awkward to be taking off her clothes in front of this woman. But Posy seemed so completely indifferent to her state of undress that Charlotte's embarrassment soon passed.

When she was seated in the tub, Posy advanced on her with a cake of soap. Mercy! Does she plan to scrub me? Charlotte thought. But Posy's ministrations were limited to washing her hair.

After that was done and Posy had carried away every stitch of the clothes she had been wearing, Charlotte finished washing herself and then remained soaking, enjoying the warmth of the water. It had been a long time since her last real bath. Back in the Mohawk Valley, a copper tub like this one had been set up in front of the kitchen fire every Saturday night. "Cleanliness is next to godliness," Mama used to say.

When the bath water had cooled, Charlotte climbed out of the tub, dried herself with the towel that Posy had left for her, and combed her hair.

She was wearing her nightgown and robe when Posy brought in the supper tray.

"Thank you," said Charlotte.

Posy nodded her head but uttered not a word. *Can't she talk?* Charlotte wondered. *Or has she been trained not to?*

On the tray lay a dish of scalloped oysters, a plate of biscuits, and an orange. There was also tea in a silver pot. To Charlotte, who had never before eaten oysters or an orange, this meal was delightfully exotic.

After she had eaten and finished getting ready for bed, she mounted a little step to climb into the deep feather bed. The combined effect of a warm bath and a good meal left Charlotte feeling much better about her plight. Even though she was not with Nick, she was ten times nearer to him than if she had stayed on Carleton Island. Very soon, she was fast asleep.

In the morning she woke to see Mrs. Knightly's head, its tresses covered by a ruffled nightcap, resting on the pillow next to hers.

When Charlotte rose, being careful not to waken Mrs. Knightly, she found her gown and cloak, well brushed, on a clothes rack. Her undergarments, washed and ironed, lay folded on a chair.

"Did Posy take good care of you?" Mrs. Knightly asked while they breakfasted in the dining room. For breakfast they ate ham served with biscuits and a strange sort of porridge that Mrs. Knightly called grits.

"Excellent care. I'm not used to such attention."

"Colonel Knightly bought Posy for me five years ago. She

was newly arrived from West Africa. He paid fifteen pounds. I thought it was too much. But Posy has proved to be worth every penny. I have trained her to arrange my hair." She touched her fingers to the artfully twined tresses. "And to look after my clothes. To my astonishment, I discovered that she was already a skilled seamstress."

"Doesn't it trouble you to keep a slave? In Africa, I suppose she was free."

Mrs. Knightly shook her head. "In Africa she was a slave to idolatry. But now she is a Christian. And so, in the life to come, she will be free."

"I was thinking of this present life."

"Servitude in this present life is a small price to pay for eternal happiness."

Charlotte gulped. It was hard to swallow the idea that Africans should be grateful to those who carried them off to a life of slavery. Even though Mrs. Knightly was more than ten years her elder and also her superior in social rank, Charlotte spoke up.

"It seems to me that you're working mighty hard to persuade yourself that something wrong is really right."

Mrs. Knightly flushed. There was a flash of anger in her eyes.

I shouldn't have said that, Charlotte thought. I'm her guest, and she's being very kind to me. But is it wrong to speak the truth, even when it's a truth she doesn't want to face?

After a silence, Mrs. Knightly said, "I forgive your impertinence. It's understandable that you share your husband's views. That being the case, you will be comfortable living in a Quaker household. And I'm happy to tell you that arrangements have been made."

"Has Colonel Knightly found a place for me to stay?"

"Yes. You will lodge with the Quaker woman I spoke of. Mrs. Doughty is a young widow with three small children to support. She is willing to take in a lodger for the few shillings a week it will bring."

Charlotte hoped that Mrs. Knightly would say that the colonel had arranged for the payment of those shillings. When she did not, Charlotte tried to think of a tactful way to raise the subject, but saw no way to do so without seeming to insult her hostess. Besides, she did not want Mrs. Knightly to think her a pauper. After all, she still had three pounds left in her purse. By being frugal, she hoped she could make them last until Nick's return.

"Who will take me to this woman's house?"

"Posy knows the way. She can take your trunk in a handcart." Mrs. Knightly pushed her chair back from the table. "I'll summon her directly."

Charlotte was waiting in the entrance hall for slaves to bring down her trunk when the front door opened and Captain Braemar stepped inside. She smiled, glad to see a familiar face.

"Good morning," he said with a bow. "I'm surprised to see you ready to go out so early. It's fortunate I haven't missed you." He reached into the black leather pouch that was attached to one of his white cross-belts. "I have a letter that Nick asked me to give you if I succeeded in meeting your ship. Rather than carry it around with me, I decided to keep it safe in my closet until you arrived."

He handed her a folded sheet of paper, closed with a red seal.

"Oh, thank you." She clutched the letter.

"I don't wish to detain you," he said, "and so I take my leave."

Charlotte cracked the letter's wax seal as soon as the door shut. She began to read:

December 6, 1780

My dearest Dear,

If you have this letter in your hands, it means that you have reached Charleston and that my friend Ralph Braemar met you. If such be the case, he will have told you the reason for my absence. Your distress at not finding me waiting can be no greater than my distress at failing you.

By now you must have learned the news that the Loyalist army raised and trained by Major Patrick Ferguson was destroyed in a battle atop a place called Kings Mountain on the 7th of October. Since then there has been great persecution of Loyalists, and it is feared that many have given up. I am being sent to the backcountry to assess morale and gauge what support for England remains.

Despite continuing strife in the rest of South Carolina, you are safe in Charleston. With eight thousand British and Loyalist troops to defend it, the rebels will not dare to attack. I trust that you will be comfortable in the officers' quarters and I hope that the pleasant society of others will divert you until my return.

She paused for a moment. If only he knew!

Before the end of February my assignment will be finished and I shall join you in Charleston—if you are in Charleston. Pardon me if I sound a little confused. The fact is, the letter I sent to stop you from setting out may have reached you in time. In that case, you aren't in Charleston anyway, and it is I who will be disappointed not to find you waiting for me.

You see by my words the state of my uncertainty. But one thing of which I am sure is my love for you. This separation is painful, but I console myself with the thought that our reunion will double and augment our joys.

A thousand kisses from your ever-loving

Nick

Before the end of February. Only a few more weeks. That wasn't so long!

Charlotte kissed the letter, refolded it, and then, reaching through the slit in the side of her gown, thrust it into her pocket. When she reached her new lodgings, she thought happily, there would be time to reread Nick's words, to ponder and to dream.

# Chapter 4

THE STREETS WERE EVEN more crowded than they had been the previous afternoon. Posy led the way, pushing the two-wheel cart ahead of her through the mire. Since the trunk was longer than the cart bed, it stuck out in front like a prow.

Another ship must have recently docked, for a surge of sailors, shouting and singing, was making its way from the direction of the wharf, no doubt to the nearest tavern. Charlotte had formed a low opinion of sailors. Their daily grog rations—four ounces of rum in the morning and four in the afternoon—seemed to keep most of them in a perpetually befuddled state.

Posy ploughed right through the crowd, as if determination could compel the sailors to fall away on either side. But they crowded even closer. Several ogled Charlotte in a most alarming manner. They were so near she could smell their sweat mingled with the rum on their breath. While she was avoiding a tattooed arm that reached out to grab her, a ragged boy bumped into her, and she staggered a little. The boy ran away without saying anything.

Once clear of the sailors, Posy and Charlotte soon reached a side street lined by small houses. Posy stopped at a plain front door. There was a window on either side of the door. The window frames, like the door, were painted grey.

"This street's called Stoll's Alley. The Quaker lady lives here."

These were the first words that Charlotte had heard Posy utter.

Charlotte rapped on the door.

After a few seconds, it opened. In the doorway stood a woman dressed in a plain black gown, without a frill or ruffle or any touch of lace. Her apron, too, was black. On her head was a black bonnet shaped like a coal scuttle, its brim so deep at both sides that it blinkered her eyes. Within the shadow of the brim, Charlotte saw determined blue eyes, clean-cut features and ivory skin. The woman's hair was so well hidden that Charlotte could not tell what the colour was. Her face, though worn, was not old. She looked about thirty years of age.

"Thee must be Mrs. Schyler. I have been expecting thee." She turned to Posy. "I'll help thee to carry the box inside."

"No! Please," said Charlotte. "Let me."

Mrs. Doughty stood aside to make way as Charlotte and Posy carried the trunk inside. After they had set it down, Charlotte reached for her pocket. Even though she needed to be careful with her money, she wanted to give Posy a penny.

The pocket was not there. Frantically she felt about in the space between her skirt and petticoat. In an instant her fingers felt the ends of the cloth tapes that had held her pocket to her belt. The tapes had been slashed.

"Oh! No!" She felt tears spring to her eyes and struggled not to cry, but this was too much.

"What's wrong?" asked Mrs. Doughty.

"My pocket is gone! My purse was in it, with all my money."

Mrs. Doughty took her hand. "Come sit down. Thee is white as a sheet."

Charlotte, her hand in Mrs. Doughty's, turned to Posy. "I'm so sorry! I wanted to give you a penny for your help."

"Them pickpockets," said Posy, "they so quick. They cut the strings and a body don't feel a thing. But never mind about giving me money. Thank you for the thought."

Posy stepped outside, picked up the handles of her cart and trundled it off down the street.

Mrs. Doughty led Charlotte to a chair, one of two plain

wooden chairs that stood in front of an empty fireplace, along with a simple wooden settle.

The room was square, with no pictures on the walls. There were no draperies at the windows—just plain shutters. The tall floor clock in its wooden case was unadorned.

Three small children were sitting on a braided rug in the centre of the room, playing with alphabet blocks. There were two little girls, about six and five years of age, and a boy of about two. Like their mother, the children wore black. Lifting their heads, they regarded Charlotte with solemn eyes.

"These are my little ones," Mrs. Doughty said. "Patience is the eldest, then Charity, and then Joseph."

"How do you do?" Charlotte hardly knew what she was saying. Her thoughts were on her stolen pocket. It wasn't just money that she had lost. Nick's letter was gone.

"Very well, I thank thee," each girl answered. Joseph merely stared.

Mrs. Doughty left the room, returning quickly with a tumbler of water.

"Thee must take such a loss with forbearance." When she handed her the water, Charlotte noticed that her hands were red and raw. "There are more important things in life than money."

Charlotte sipped the water. "Important or not, money is necessary if I am to pay for my lodging."

"Let's not worry about that."

"I don't like to be beholden."

"Since thee has no money, I welcome thee not as a lodger but as a guest."

"But I can't accept your hospitality without giving anything in return. There must be something I can do to help you."

"Do not fret. I do it for thy husband's sake. Nick is a friend, though not a friend."

This curious statement caught Charlotte's attention. "A friend but not a friend?"

"Others call us Quakers, but the Society of Friends is what we call ourselves. Thy husband shares our beliefs about war and slavery."

"Nick is a man of peace. That's why he served as a courier but never as a soldier."

"It's hard to preach peace in a time of war. For the most part, we Friends are tolerated. But our situation has worsened of late, as much because of our abhorrence of slavery as because of our hatred of bloodshed. My husband Caleb was fined because I taught a black girl to read and write."

"Is that against the law?"

"It is. And the law assumes that whatever a wife does, she does it under her husband's direction."

"I did know that. My father says that the men who made that law must all have been bachelors."

"In this case, my husband approved of what I did, and he said so when he appeared before the magistrate. The magistrate rebuked him severely. But being fined didn't change our ways. In fact, it made our opposition to slavery stronger still. We resolved to buy a slave in order to set him free. It took a year of frugal living to save enough money. Thirty pounds was the price. The slave's name was Duncan. He went north to New York, where it would be easier for him to live as a free man.

"Caleb knew he would pay a price for giving Duncan his freedom. When he lost a third of his customers, he was not surprised. We were both prepared for that."

As she spoke, Mrs. Doughty's fingers were twisting a corner of her apron. "One week after Duncan left, ruffians attacked Caleb on his way home from a meeting of the Friends." She raised the corner of the apron to her eyes. "A neighbour found him and brought him home." A sob caught in her throat. "Caleb did not survive."

For a moment Charlotte could not speak. When she did speak, "I'm so sorry," was all she could say. Her sympathy was mixed with horror. This man had been murdered for his decent, courageous human act.

Mrs. Doughty gave a quick look at her children. She sat up straight in her chair, and Charlotte saw that she was determined to compose herself. She doesn't want to upset her children, Charlotte thought.

"Caleb was a shoemaker, a good provider," Mrs. Doughty continued in a quiet voice. "His death brought us close to ruin. But the Friends help us. And I carry on my husband's work."

She raised her head. "Now I must make thee welcome in our home. The two bedrooms upstairs are where my children and I sleep. The best I can offer thee is a cot in the kitchen."

"Mrs. Doughty, for three weeks I slept in a greasy hammock, slung from hooks in the ship's timbers. Before that, my bed was two flour sacks sewn together and stuffed with beech leaves. So you see, a cot in your kitchen will suit me fine."

More than fine, she said to herself. But she must find some way to contribute. Only then could she feel perfectly comfortable living here.

Looking around the Quaker family's simple home, she thought it was a good place to wait for Nick's return. But what did Mrs. Doughty mean by saying that she carried on her husband's work? Her husband had been a shoemaker. There was no sign of cobbler's tools about. So she couldn't mean that.

# Chapter 5

THE FIRST THINGS Charlotte noticed in Mrs. Doughty's kitchen were half-a-dozen clotheslines stretching from wall to wall overhead. Apart from that, the kitchen was much like any other. It held a wooden table, a counter with a dry sink, a slop bucket under the sink, and shelves above the counter. There was a fireplace for cooking, with a swing-out crane from which pots could be hung. Near the back door stood a big copper washtub on an iron stand. In the washtub, red, green, blue, and brown clothes were soaking in sudsy water. There seemed to be clothes of every colour except Quaker black.

"Would thee like a biscuit?" Mrs. Doughty asked. "I made them fresh this morning."

"No, thank you. I breakfasted well."

"Then I'll get back to my work." She rolled up her sleeves, pulled a green shirt from the water, and began to rub it vigorously on her scrubbing board.

"May I help?" asked Charlotte.

"Only one person can use a scrub board at a time. But thee can keep me company." She wrung out the shirt and laid it on a wooden trough that stood next to the tub. "I should like to know more about thee, if I may."

"Of course." Charlotte sat down at the kitchen table. "I was born and raised on a farm near a little place called Fort Hunter in the Mohawk Valley."

She fell silent as memories flooded her mind. The warm kitchen with its long harvest table. The smell of earth in the spring, just after the ploughing was done. The honking of wild geese passing overhead on wide-spread wings.

Mrs. Doughty lifted her head. "Go on."

"I had three brothers." Charlotte fought the lump in her throat that always rose when she thought of the loved ones she had lost. "There was James, then came Charlie, and then Isaac. I'm the youngest, born five years after Isaac. We were a happy family until the year I turned thirteen. That's when everything changed. There was talk of revolution. People took sides. They were either Tories, like my family, loyal to England, or they were Whigs, ready to fight for independence. Neighbours who'd been our friends now became enemies."

"It was the same in the Carolinas."

"I think it was like that everywhere." Charlotte paused. "All three of my brothers were killed."

Mrs. Doughty stopped scrubbing. "All three were killed?"

"James and Charlie died at the Battle of Saratoga. A week later, a Liberty man shot Isaac. There was so much violence in the Mohawk Valley that Papa said we had to leave. We made our way north to Canada. There we took refuge at Fort Haldimand on Carleton Island, at the eastern end of Lake Ontario. We lived in the Loyalist refugee camp. Our only shelter was a tent."

"Even in winter? It must have been terrible."

"It was terrible. The second winter, Mama died." Charlotte swallowed hard. "I don't think I can talk about this any more."

"I will not press thee further." Mrs. Doughty lifted another garment from the tub, wrung it, and placed it on the trough. "Only this: where did thee meet Nick? Was it on Carleton Island?"

"I knew him long before that. We were both pupils at Sir William Johnson's school at Fort Hunter. There were thirty of us, little ones in the front rows, big ones in the back. I started school when I was seven. Nick was one of the big boys. Ten years old. He stood out because he was always asking questions—not to show off, but because he wanted to know the 'why' about everything."

"Then he hasn't changed." Mrs. Doughty laid another garment on the trough.

"I don't think he ever will. After he turned fourteen and

was finished school, I'd see him drop by to borrow books from the schoolmaster. There was one called *Gulliver's Travels* and another called *Candide* that he talked about. But it was much later that he told me about the books, when I was fifteen and we were courting."

"When Nick first came to Charleston," said Mrs. Doughty, "he attended our meetings a few times. That's how my husband and I met him. He was respectful of our beliefs, but he could not accept all of them. Reason, he said, was his only guide."

"He has told me the same," said Charlotte.

"Reason should not be our only guide, but it guided Nick to two great truths: slavery is wrong and war is wrong." She stood up. "Now, if thee will help me empty the tub and fill it with fresh water, I can rinse the clothes. Then we'll hang them to dry." She glanced out the window. "It's a fair day. They'll dry quickly in the breeze."

Later, as they were pegging the laundry onto the clotheslines in the backyard, Mrs. Doughty said, "I have an idea how thee can help me. I take in washing from five households. To pick it up and deliver it is the hardest part of my work. I have to carry the bundle of laundry through the streets while keeping an eye on three little children. Then the children need to be cleaned up when we return home."

"I understand that. The streets are foul."

"People dump their garbage and empty their chamber pots right onto the roadway. Though they're fined if caught in the act, many do it anyway."

"I'll be happy to pick up and deliver laundry, for I want very much to make some contribution."

"That's settled, then. I have a spare pocket I can give thee. Thee will need it to collect payment."

"Thank you. I'll guard it more carefully than the one stolen from me." She paused. "I don't want to be impolite, but may I ask you a question?"

"Thee answered my questions. Why should I not answer thine?"

"It's about the way you talk."

"We call it plain speech."

"It's not like the Bible. You don't say 'thou.' Just 'thee.'"

"Plain speech has its own rules. 'Thee' is correct for speaking to one person. We use 'you' when speaking to two or more. We believe that to say 'you' when speaking to one person is to acknowledge that person as your superior in rank. We Friends observe no distinctions of rank. To us, all are equal."

"I see," said Charlotte, who really did not see but wanted to be respectful.

"We use plain speech to remind ourselves of who and what we are."

"Then you don't mind if I talk the way I'm used to?"

"Not in the least."

That evening when the light was fading, Mrs. Doughty lit a candle, closed the kitchen window shutters, and then went into the front room to close the shutters there.

"We retire early to save on candles," Mrs. Doughty said, "and we rise at daybreak. The kitchen fire will give enough light for thee to see thy way to bed."

"I wish you good night," Charlotte said.

Mrs. Doughty stopped at the bottom of the narrow stairs that ascended from the kitchen. "In the morning, if thee wants to write a letter to thy father, I'll give thee pen and paper."

"Thank you, Mrs. Doughty. But there's no way a letter can reach him in winter. It will be April before the ice breaks up so that a bateau can travel up the St. Lawrence River to Carleton Island."

"He must worry about thee."

"I know he does. Since Mama died, I'm all he has."

"I shall remember him in my prayers."

After Mrs. Doughty had shepherded her children upstairs, Charlotte changed into her nightgown, the one she had bought to please Nick.

Where was Nick now? she wondered as she lay on the cot under a patchwork quilt. If only she had his letter to read over again! Charlotte squeezed her eyes shut and tried to visualize the words on the page. Nick had called her "my dearest Dear." He had said that his assignment would be completed by the end of February. He had promised her a thousand kisses. Now *that* was something to look forward to! She just had to concentrate on those kisses and not let herself think of the dangers he faced before she could collect them. Thinking about Nick, she drifted happily into sleep.

A cry startled her awake. She stiffened, but did not move. It sounded like the squawky wail of a very young baby. She could not place where it came from, and listened to hear it again. But all was silence. I must have been dreaming, she decided, and went back to sleep.

In the morning she told Mrs. Doughty what she thought she had heard.

An alarmed expression crossed the woman's face, but her voice was composed. "It could have been a dream. Or a noise in the street."

"It must have been," Charlotte said. But it hadn't felt like a dream, and the cry had sounded too close to have come from the street.

# Chapter 6

AFTER BREAKFAST, Mrs. Doughty wrapped in a canvas sheet the clothes that she had washed the previous day. She tied the bundle with cords.

"I've drawn thee a map." She showed Charlotte a piece of paper. "Here's Stoll's Alley, where we are now. Thee must take this bundle to Mrs. Edgar, on King Street. I've marked the house with an X."

"I'll find it," Charlotte said, looking at the X.

"The charge is three shillings. Be sure Mrs. Edgar pays thee. Don't let her put thee off by saying she'll pay next week." Mrs. Doughty placed the bundle in Charlotte's arms. "When thee returns, thee will find the door unlocked."

Was she wise to leave the door unlocked? Charlotte won-dered as she started out. With footpads and drunken sailors roaming the streets, surely this was folly. Or was it faith that God would watch over her home? If so, Mrs. Doughty should place less reliance on God and more on common sense.

The bundle was awkward to carry, though not especially heavy. The difficulty was keeping her footing. With every step her shoes squelched in slimy muck.

With the map to guide her, Charlotte easily found Mrs. Edgar's home. The front door, like that of many Charleston houses, opened onto a long veranda that ran along the side of the house. Without setting down her bundle, Charlotte managed to scrape her muddy shoes on the bootjack before setting foot on the spotless veranda floor. Halfway along the veranda was the actual entrance to the house.

At Charlotte's knock, a black woman opened the door and held out her arms to receive the load. In her flower-print dress and white apron, she looked neat and tidy enough to be the lady of the house. Only her colour told a different story.

"The charge is three shillings," Charlotte said, not releas-ing the bundle.

"I'll fetch my mistress."

Standing with the laundry in her arms, Charlotte waited several minutes before a stern-faced white woman came to the door. A white, ruffled cap covered her hair, and she wore a calico gown.

"You could have given the laundry to my slave." Her cold

voice made her annoyance clear.

"I expected you'd want to pay me yourself." Charlotte felt emboldened, ready for battle.

Mrs. Edgar looked her up and down. Charlotte's well-made blue cloak with its braid trim was a garment no Quaker would wear and no washerwoman could afford.

"It's not convenient just now," said Mrs. Edgar. "I'll pay next week."

Charlotte drew back, still holding the bundle.

Mrs. Edgar sighed. "Let me get my purse. Two shillings, isn't it?"

"Three."

With the money tucked safely into her new pocket, Charlotte felt pleased with herself. The walk back to Stoll's Alley seemed no great distance at all.

She had nearly reached Mrs. Doughty's front door when she noticed a big man standing in the shadow of a doorway across the street, staring at the house. Although the brim of his hat shadowed his face, she could see that he was white. He had a thick neck, his shoulders sloped, and his shape was so bulky he made her think of a bear. When he noticed Charlotte looking at him, he turned his head away, as if his interest were in something further down the street.

"Did all go well?" Mrs. Doughty looked up from the kitchen table, where she was kneading dough on a floured board.

"Perfectly well. Mrs. Edgar made almost no objection to paying." Retrieving the coins from her pocket, Charlotte placed them on the table. "But there's one thing I should tell you. A man is watching your house. He's there right now, standing in the doorway across the street."

Mrs. Doughty flinched. After wiping her hands, she went into the front room, stopping close to the window, but not so close that anyone could see her from across the street.

"I have seen that man before." She turned to Charlotte. "This house is often watched. None of my neighbours belong to the Society of Friends. Many have held me in suspicion ever since I was caught teaching a slave to read."

"You were brave to do that."

"Not especially brave. It began almost by accident." Mrs. Doughty turned away from the window and returned to the kitchen. As she went back to kneading the lump of dough, she began to tell the story. Charlotte sat down to listen.

"The girl's name was Phoebe. She was twelve years old. My husband rented her at the time of my last lying in."

"Rented her!"

"It's quite common. Some people purchase slaves for the sole purpose of renting them out. It's an investment. For example, a family wanting an addition built onto to their house will pay a good price to rent a skilled carpenter. In my case, I needed somebody to help with housework and to take care of Patience and Charity.

"I had been ill with yellow fever in the first months of my pregnancy and was still not strong. Some Friends criticized my husband for renting a slave, until they realized that I needed more help than they could give.

"Phoebe was very bright. Her mistress, Mrs. Morley, was training her to be a household servant, and so she had taught her to sew and to speak correct English, unlike the Gullah dialect field workers use. Phoebe lived with us for eight months. Since Mrs. Morley had gone to England to visit relatives, Phoebe was not needed in their household during that time.

"When I gave birth to Joseph, Patience was four and Charity was three. Patience had a set of alphabet blocks, with which she'd learned to spell a few words. One day I sat nearby, holding Joseph in my arms, while she tried to teach her sister to spell 'Charity.' Phoebe, who was watching, said, 'Can you make my name?' Patience answered that she would try, and she spelled it as 'F-e-e-b-e-e.'"

Charlotte smiled.

Mrs. Doughty continued. "'Very good,' I said. 'But not quite correct.' I then explained about 'PH' and 'F' making the same sound. I laid Joseph in his cradle, got down on the rug with them, and showed them the right spelling. Then I used the blocks to spell more words. From then on, Phoebe was making words with those blocks whenever she had a free minute. I gave her a quill and paper and showed her how to form letters. Then I taught her to read Bible verses. By the time she left us, she could read just about anything. That was two years ago."

"I wonder how many books she's had a chance to read

since then?" said Charlotte. "Not many, I reckon."

"Her mistress caught her reading one—a novel that had been left on a table. Its title was *Fanny's Garters*. A foolish, wicked book, or so I've heard. I was shocked to learn that Phoebe would fill her head with such trash."

"Was Phoebe punished?"

"I believe she escaped with a warning. At that time, she was a favourite with Mrs. Morley."

At that time? But perhaps not now? Charlotte wished that Mrs. Doughty would explain, but it seemed she had nothing to add to the story.

In the afternoon, she asked Charlotte to go to another address to pick up laundry for washing the next day.

This time, Charlotte put on her old gown and cloak, as they seemed more suited to her work. It gave her a glad feeling to have a useful task. And picking up dirty laundry was certainly no worse than mucking out a barn, which had been one of her chores on the family farm.

As she closed the door behind her, Charlotte saw that the big white man still lurked in the shadow of the doorway across the street, and, further up the block, a black boy was also watching the house. He was young, of average height, and he had a thin, wiry build. His shirt was torn, his feet bare, and his breeches stained. The boy's eyes met hers for a moment, and then he ran away, disappearing down a narrow passage between two houses.

This is strange, Charlotte thought. Two people watching—one white and one black. Why should either be spying on the house of a simple Quaker family?

Upon returning with the load of dirty laundry, she said to Mrs. Doughty, "I think someone else is keeping an eye on the house. He's black, and he looks about fifteen years old."

"Oh." Mrs. Doughty's eyes met Charlotte's for an instant, and then she turned her head away.

Charlotte had the feeling that Mrs. Doughty wanted to tell her something, that she was on the verge but had not decided yet.

# Chapter 7

A SCREAM CUT through her slumber.

A woman's scream. Then a baby's ragged cry. In an instant Charlotte was bolt upright, her body ready to act though sleep still blurred her mind.

Another scream. It came from the front room.

Then a crash, like a chair knocked over. Charlotte sprang from her cot and ran toward the noise. In the darkness, all she could see was the tall rectangle of the front doorway, open to the night. Framed in that paler darkness two figures struggled, a man and a woman. The man, big like a bear, was dragging the woman from the house. Over and over she screamed, "Let me go! Let me go!" It didn't sound like Mrs. Doughty's voice.

Men were shouting in the street.

A baby was crying.

Charlotte raced toward the door, when suddenly there was no floor beneath her feet. She was falling, tumbling. Her body bounced. Hip, spine, shoulder. She landed hard. Her head snapped back, struck something, and rang like a bell.

For a long moment the ringing in Charlotte's ears drowned every other noise. Then the ringing stopped. The screaming and shouting sounded far away. But the crying baby was very near. Its wails filled the dank air.

If this was a nightmare, she wanted to wake up now.

Above her, footsteps thumped. Over the baby's wailing, she heard Mrs. Doughty's voice. "Charlotte! Charlotte!"

A candle flame appeared overhead, and behind the flame Mrs. Doughty's blurred features. She was looking down over the edge of a big, square hole. By the candle's light Charlotte saw a set of steep, narrow steps.

"I'm down here." Now she realized what had happened. She had fallen through a trap door. She was lying in a cellar. The existence of either a trap door or a cellar had never crossed her mind. Her head pounded. The baby's cries echoed all around.

So the woman being dragged away couldn't have been Mrs. Doughty. Some other woman. Who? And what had she been doing in this house?

Mrs. Doughty was descending the stairs. Charlotte considered rolling out of the way, but before she could manage it, Mrs. Doughty stepped over her and knelt at her side.

"Is thee hurt?"

"A bit shaken."

"That's no wonder!"

"What's going on? There's a baby . . . and a woman . . ."

"I'm sorry! I should have told thee all."

The baby was still crying. Charlotte turned her head. Now by the candle's flickering light she saw a cradle on the cellar floor. The noise was coming from that cradle. Sobbing, choking—a baby in distress.

So it was neither a dream nor a noise in the street that she had heard the previous night. There was a baby in the house.

Mrs. Doughty set down the candlestick on a step. From the cradle she lifted the wailing infant. It was small. Not much bigger than a cat.

"There, there," Mrs. Doughty murmured, patting the baby's back, "that's my brave little man!" The baby quieted after a few gulping sobs. Rocking him in her arms, she looked down at Charlotte, who still lay sprawled at the bottom of the stairs. "I'm sorry I failed to tell thee about the baby. It was both wrong and foolish to hide the truth from thee."

"It doesn't matter. Just tell me what's going on. Who was that woman?"

"Phoebe, the girl I taught to read."

"And that baby is her child?"

"Yes."

"And the white man who's been watching your house is the one who dragged her away?"

"The slave catcher. Yes."

Although her head ached, Charlotte's brain was beginning to put the puzzle together.

"What about the black boy who was watching the house?"

"His name is Jammy. The Morley family owns him as well as Phoebe. Jammy's the stable groom."

"Is he the baby's father?"

"No. He's not the father." Mrs. Doughty paused. "Let me take the baby upstairs and then come back for thee. A dark cellar is no place to talk."

Now that the baby was quiet, Patience, Charity and Joseph began a crying chorus of their own, the noise carrying from their upstairs bedroom down to the cellar. What a night for everyone!

Mrs. Doughty carried the baby up the steep steps. She would not return for quite a while, Charlotte thought, not until she had managed to settle all the little ones.

Charlotte moved her limbs one by one. Nothing felt seriously wrong. Putting her hand to the back of her head, she felt a bump, but no bleeding. No need to wait for Mrs. Doughty's help. Bringing the candle with her, she crept up the steep steps.

At the top, she sat for a moment on the floor near the open trap door. She had better close it, she thought, before anybody else fell through.

The door moved freely on its hinges. When she had it closed, she went into the kitchen to rekindle the fire. The baby, wrapped in a blanket, was asleep on top of the quilt that covered Charlotte's cot, where Mrs. Doughty had laid him down.

From above came the voice of Mrs. Doughty comforting her children.

When the fire was blazing, Charlotte filled the kettle and hung it on the hook over the flames. They could use a cup of tea while they talked, and they certainly did need to talk. Charlotte suspected that some terrible trouble lay behind the events of the night.

After a time, Mrs. Doughty came downstairs and collapsed onto a chair at the table. Charlotte poured the tea and passed a cup to her.

"Who is the baby's father? Or doesn't it matter?"

"It matters."

Charlotte waited, expecting she knew not what.

Mrs. Morley set down her teacup. Her eyes met Charlotte's.

"The father is Phoebe's master, Lewis Morley. He forced himself upon her. She was fourteen."

"Oh!" For a moment, silence hung between them. "That's terrible."

She didn't know what else to say. She had been prepared for something bad, but not as bad as this. It was sad. It was sordid. It appeared to be dangerous. Mrs. Doughty had answered her question, yet the answer just raised more questions. Although Charlotte dreaded what she would hear next, she wanted to know the truth.

"It's common," Mrs. Doughty said, "for a master to abuse his female slaves. They have no power against him."

"Common? If the slave owner is married, doesn't his wife object?"

"The wives can't stop it. Most pretend not to notice. Some accept it as a normal part of married life."

"Merciful heavens! What can they be thinking?"

"They must accept what they cannot change. Mrs. Morley, like many wives in her situation, can't stand the sight of her husband's half-black children. The more they resemble him, the more bitter she feels."

"I don't blame her."

"Mrs. Morley will not allow such children to remain in the household. Phoebe knew that her baby would soon be taken from her. Rather then lose him, she decided to run away with him, and she turned to Jammy for help."

"He agreed to help her?"

"Yes. Jammy adores her." Mrs. Doughty raised the cup to her lips, sipped, and then set it down. "Their plan was for me to hide Phoebe and the baby while Jammy looked for contacts to help them flee north. There's slavery up north too, but it's not as common. And the further away they went, the safer they'd be from slave catchers."

"So you offered to help them?"

"Not exactly. It was a complete surprise when they showed up at my door last week. I hadn't seen Phoebe for two years. She had the baby in her arms. 'Phoebe,' I said to her, 'my house is the first place slave catchers are going to look.' But she begged so piteously I hadn't the heart to turn her away.

"Jammy helped me to set up a hiding place in the cellar, with a mattress for Phoebe and Joseph's old cradle for the baby. I told him that my door would remain unlocked day and night until he managed to take Phoebe and the baby away."

"I thought it strange that you didn't lock your door," said Charlotte. "There are so many footpads and drunken sailors around. But now I understand."

"From the start, I saw slave catchers watching my house. After a few more days, I saw Jammy watching too. I hoped this meant he'd found somebody to help them and was waiting for a chance to take Phoebe and the baby away."

"Then I arrived," said Charlotte, "to complicate matters."

"Thy arrival surely caused a problem. To reject Colonel Knightly's offer would have raised questions, since everybody knew I needed money. It was foolish to imagine that I could keep thee from knowing there was a baby in the house. I should have told thee about Phoebe at the beginning."

"I reckon you wanted first to know me better."

"No. I trusted thee from the start. But I didn't want to bring trouble upon thee. It's a crime to help a slave escape. In the eyes of the law, concealing a crime makes one a party to it. If I could keep Phoebe's presence a secret, thee would not be put in that position.

"For the past three nights I've scarce slept a wink. Tonight

I heard the hinges squeak when Jammy opened the trap door, and then the uproar when the slave catchers burst in. There were two of them. One took Jammy. The other took Phoebe."

"But they left the baby."

"They had their hands full with Jammy and Phoebe."

"Do you think they'll come back for the baby?"

"Not likely. The Morleys don't want him. As for selling him, a one-month-old infant wouldn't fetch enough to pay the slave catcher's fee. For the present at least, the baby is ours to care for."

"In that case," Charlotte said, "let's bring the cradle up from the cellar. There are still a few hours left before dawn. After some sleep, we can think more clearly what to do."

Standing up, Charlotte felt dizzy. Her head hurt badly while she helped Mrs. Doughty haul the wooden cradle up the stairs and set it near the kitchen fireplace. The sleeping baby did not wake when Mrs. Doughty lifted him from the cot and tucked him in the cradle.

Now all was quiet. Charlotte lay down on her cot, but she could not stop worrying about Phoebe, Jammy and the baby. Light was visible through the crack between the shutters before she drifted off.

# Chapter 8

IN THE MORNING Mrs. Doughty went out in search of a wet nurse, confident that she could find among the Friends a nursing mother who would want to help.

A heap of laundry was waiting to be done. Charlotte filled the washtub with hot water and set to work. She felt better now, her headache gone. The baby was in his cradle in the kitchen. The front room rug was back in place, hiding the trap door. Patience, Charity and Joseph were sitting on it, playing with little spinning toys she had made, one for each of them, from a button and a string.

Charlotte added her delicate nightgown to the clothes in the washtub. Her fall into the cellar, landing her on the dirt floor, had left the fabric embedded with grime. She scrubbed and scrubbed, although she knew that no matter how hard she tried, it would never be so fresh and pretty as before. But the state of a nightgown, she reminded herself, was unimportant when compared with the plight of Phoebe, Jammy, and the now motherless baby.

She was rinsing the clothes when Mrs. Doughty returned.

"I've found a wet nurse. Her name is Hannah Perkins. She can't keep the baby in her home, because she has her own little ones to care for. I would like thee to take him to her twice every day. Friend Perkins lives on Meeting Street. I'll give thee directions."

"Will two feedings be enough?" Charlotte knew enough about babies to realize that they were hungry nearly all the time.

"He won't think so," Mrs. Doughty said wryly. "We'll have to comfort him with sugar water in between."

"When shall I take him there?"

"Take him now. I'll finish the laundry. He'll want a feeding as soon as he wakes."

Charlotte bent over the cradle and picked up the baby. She was surprised at his weight. He was much more solid than he looked, a real flesh-and-blood little person with tawny skin and a fuzz of black hair.

"What's his name? You never mentioned a name."

"Noah."

He woke as she was wrapping him in a shawl, staring up at her with wide grey eyes. She took a second look.

"His eyes are grey!"

"He has his father's eyes."

Mr. Morley's eyes.

"Then it's no wonder his presence made Mrs. Morley uncomfortable. If I were Mrs. Morley, I wouldn't like it either." Charlotte paused. "What about Phoebe? Those grey eyes must remind her every single day of what her master did to her. Frankly, I don't understand how she can love this baby so much. I don't think I could love a child born as the result of such a deed."

"If thee lived Phoebe's life, thee might understand. Her mother is a field hand at a rice plantation owned by Mrs. Morley's brother-in-law Paul Vesey, twenty miles up the Cooper River. Five years ago, when Mrs. Morley was looking for a bright girl to train up as a house servant, her sister, Mrs. Vesey, said she could have Phoebe as a birthday present. She was ten years old when Mrs. Morley brought her to Charleston, a frightened child torn away from everyone she loved. Phoebe hasn't seen her mother or her brothers and sisters since. This baby makes up for everything she's lost."

"She has Jammy."

"And she loves him, but in a different way. They've been friends ever since the Morleys brought Phoebe to Charleston. And lately . . . they're more than friends. The Morleys bought Jammy when he was six years old to be trained as a stable groom. He slept in the stable. According to Phoebe, his only friends were horses until she joined the household. Phoebe tells me they want to spend their lives together. But then, they're both only fifteen. Who knows what will happen?"

The baby, whose big grey eyes had been fixed on Charlotte's face for several minutes, began to pucker his lips and suckle at the air.

"Be off with thee," said Mrs. Doughty. "We've done enough talking. This little one's hunger can't be denied."

Friend Perkins was a plump, cheerful woman whose coal-scuttle bonnet was askew and apron far from spotless. She had two little children clinging to her and a few larger ones trailing after. There were so many she made Charlotte think of the old woman who lived in a shoe.

As soon as Friend Perkins saw Noah, she took him into her arms, gave him a cuddle, and pronounced him a perfect angel.

"Will thee step inside and have a seat for half an hour while he feeds?" she asked.

Charlotte, seeing nowhere in the front room to sit down without displacing a child, decided that this was a good opportunity to go for a walk.

It was a bright, clear morning. She decided to stroll down to the wharves on the Cooper River to watch the ships until it was time to pick up Noah.

After Charlotte had finished her walk and taken Noah back to Stoll's Alley, Mrs. Doughty had another task for her. It was time to pick up the load of laundry for washing the next day.

"Keep thine ears and eyes open when thee goes about town," said Mrs. Doughty. "News travels fast in Charleston. There may be talk about last night."

"I'll do my best, for I'd surely like to know what's happened to Jammy and Phoebe."

It was mid-afternoon. The sky had clouded over since earlier in the day and a chilly wind was blowing from the harbour.

The customer's slave woman had the laundry bundle ready. Handing it over in a businesslike manner, she showed no inclination to chat.

The laundry bundle was large and awkward to carry. Charlotte's arms and shoulders strained under its weight, and she could hardly see over it or around it. What a sad sight she must present, she thought, wearing her shabby gown and carrying a load of dirty laundry. At least she was unlikely to meet anyone she knew. That was something to be thankful for.

Her gown had been a good one once. She had worn it on the trek north when her family had fled from the Mohawk Valley, and it had served her for three years in the Loyalist camp on Carleton Island. Now, its deep blue faded to nondescript grey, it made her look like any poor washerwoman on her rounds.

And this was a good thing because, if she wanted to listen for gossip, she must be inconspicuous.

At a street corner, three redcoats stood chatting. Perhaps

they were discussing last night's ruckus in the street. Affecting a weary manner, she approached as closely as she dared and leaned against a lamppost, as if needing its support.

The soldiers were not talking about slaves or slave catchers. Their subject was a recent battle fought at a place called Cowpens.

Cowpens! It sounded like a barnyard, not a battlefield.

Apparently Cowpens was a place in the backcountry where the rebels had recently defeated an army of British and Loyalist troops. The three redcoats assured each other that this was just a minor setback. As they discussed the battle, it became clear to Charlotte that their conversation would shed no light upon slave catcher activities last night. She walked on.

The next place she stopped was in front of a coffee house, where two periwigged gentlemen in frockcoats stood chatting in the doorway. One sported a dark green coat. The other's coat was navy blue.

She bent her head to listen.

The gentlemen were criticizing England's policy regarding slaves. It wasn't that either of them supported the revolution. Certainly not! God save the King! But to arm escaped slaves was dangerous. Who knew when they might turn upon the very people who set them free?

This conversation sounded promising. She waited and, sure enough, in a few moments she heard a word she had been waiting for.

"Jammy."

Charlotte trudged over to the wall, leaned against it, and heaved a weary sigh. If the gentlemen noticed her, they would think she was simply resting for a minute and not paying attention to them at all.

"The boy's run away three times," said the gentleman in green. "He'll hang when they catch him. He overpowered the slave catcher, knocked him senseless, and ran away shouting, 'Phoebe, I'm comin' back for you!' The other slave catcher was so busy hanging on to the girl that he couldn't help his partner. But he heard what the boy said."

The gentleman in the blue coat laughed out loud. "'Phoebe, I'm comin' back for you!'" he repeated in a mocking tone. "Noble sentiments . . . for a slave. So when Jammy returns to rescue the damsel in distress, they'll put a rope around his neck."

"Damn shame. I'm sorry for Lewis," said his companion. "He told me the boy's a first-rate hand with horses. A good stable groom is hard to find. But Lewis has to make an example of him or we'll end up with a full-scale slave revolt. At least they got back the girl."

"The Morleys aren't keeping her, though," said the gentleman in the blue coat. "I met Lewis this morning on his way to the *Royal Gazette* office to place an advertisement. The wench will be sold at auction next week."

"I'm not surprised they've decided to sell her," said the other. "Lewis' wife Abby told my wife months ago that the girl was giving her a lot of trouble. This was even before that awkward business of the baby. Abby said the girl is too clever for her own good. A couple of years ago, the Morleys hired her out to a Quaker woman who taught her to read and write. That's what spoiled her."

"Quite right," said the gentleman in blue. "A slave's no good once he gets a little learning into his head. Turns him into a troublemaker. Best thing the Morleys can do with the girl is sell her."

"Those Quakers are a serious problem we need to deal with," said the gentleman in the green coat. "For all their peaceful ways, they're a threat to society. If our slaves someday rise up against us, the Quakers will have our blood on their hands."

Now Charlotte had some real news. Jammy was a fugitive. Phoebe had been returned to her owners and was about to be sold.

Tightening her arms around her bundle, she set off for Stoll's Alley.

# Chapter 9

THE HARBOUR WIND whipped at her back. It had started to rain, and the muck underfoot was slippery. Peering around the edge of her bundle, she looked for solid footing where there was none. She just hoped she could get back to Stoll's Alley without taking a tumble.

It was not to be. Stepping around a pile of horse manure, she skidded and landed on her backside. For a moment she simply sat there, the bundle still in her arms. Well, she thought, it's a good thing I'm carrying dirty laundry instead of clean.

A stout man wearing a tricorn hat walked by, looking away in an obvious pretence that he did not see her. Charlotte was still sitting on the muddy roadway when she noticed some-one coming from across the street. He stopped in front of her.

"Allow me to help you."

He spoke with a Mohawk Valley accent, not the drawn-out South Carolina drawl. Charlotte recognized more than just the accent. She knew the voice. Looking up, she saw a red coat with white cross belts, and above the coat the famil-iar face of her friend Elijah Cobman, formerly of the King's Royal Regiment of New York, the Royal Greens.

Their eyes met. His jaw dropped.

"Charlotte!"

"Oh, Elijah!" She felt as overwhelmed as if her guardian angel had appeared before her, totally forgetting that she did not want to encounter anyone she knew. But Elijah was dif-ferent—a friend with whom she had shared danger and hardship.

"Are you hurt?"

"I don't think so."

He held out his hand to help her.

"Please. Just take the bundle. Then I can get up on my own."

He took it from her and held it while she struggled to her feet. The bundle was only slightly splashed with muck; Char-lotte's gown was a mess.

Elijah stared at her in a dazed sort of way. "What are you doing here? When I saw you on Carleton Island three months ago, you never breathed a word about going to Charleston, even when I told you the army might send me back down south."

"Three months ago, I hadn't the least idea. I got a letter from Nick just a few days after you left. In his letter Nick told me he was no longer a courier. He said Southern Command had transferred him to a different department and given him a room in the officers' quarters. So he wanted me to come to Charleston to join him."

"That sounds mighty fine."

"It would have been mighty fine, except they cancelled his transfer. I didn't know a thing about it until I arrived in Charleston and was told he'd been sent on a mission to the backcountry. So I'm here, but Nick is not."

Elijah gave a sympathetic smile. "When I first met you, you were waiting for Nick to find you, and now you're waiting for him again. There always seems to be something keeping you two apart."

He watched while she twisted and tugged at her clothing, trying to see how dirty it was at the back.

"I can carry your bundle for you, wherever you're going."

"Thank you. I'd appreciate that, if you don't mind being seen with me."

"Not at all. This reminds me of how we met. Remember Canajoharie? You were peering into our kitchen window, mud all over the back of your gown, just like now."

"Same gown," she laughed. "Different mud."

"You were looking for a place where your family could hide after the Sons of Liberty ran you off your farm. I thought you were a rebel spy."

"You came up behind me with a pitchfork and steered me to the front door. Your mother took one look and said, 'That's the dirtiest spy I ever seen.'"

He laughed. "You have a talent for landing in mud."

"And you have a talent for rescuing me."

"What's the reason this time? What are you doing, walking around in the rain, carrying that big bundle?"

"The bundle is dirty clothes, and I'm taking it to the place where I lodge, the home of a Quaker woman who takes in laundry."

"Didn't you just say that Nick had a room in the officers' quarters?"

"He did. But when Southern Command cancelled his transfer, they gave his room to somebody else. Since they couldn't throw me out on the street, they arranged for me to lodge with Mrs. Doughty."

"So you're living with Quakers. That's quite a change."

"I liked the idea because I thought it would be peaceful and quiet."

"Isn't it?"

"Not at all. As I soon discovered, Mrs. Doughty had a runaway slave girl with a baby hiding in the cellar. I didn't know this until slave catchers invaded the house."

Charlotte paused, wondering if she should tell Elijah the

details of Phoebe's plight. But, no. It was unnecessary.

"Go on," he said.

"The slave catchers captured the girl but left the baby. So now we have a baby to take care of."

They reached Stoll's Alley and stopped at Mrs. Doughty's door.

"Would you like to come in," Charlotte asked, "and meet Mrs. Doughty?"

"I wish I could. But I'm due back at barracks." A shadow passed over his face. "I very much want to talk with you."

"I'd like that. Then you can tell me everything that's happened to you since the army sent you back down south."

"Maybe tomorrow?"

"Tomorrow will be fine. But there's no rush, is there? If you're attached to the garrison, you'll be in Charleston for a while." She pressed the door latch.

"I think not." He frowned. "Look. There hasn't been anybody here I can talk to. But I can talk to you. I can talk to you about anything."

"Are you in trouble?"

They looked directly into each other's eyes, and then he turned away.

"No. Not yet. I mean . . ." He spoke in a rush. "Oh, I don't know what I mean. That is . . . ever since the Battle of Kings Mountain. So many died there."

"Come tomorrow. I have errands in the morning and afternoon. But I'm here around noon."

"Noon, then." He passed the laundry bundle into her arms.

Maybe he isn't in trouble, she thought as she watched him turn and walk away, but something heavy weighs upon his mind.

She opened the door and stepped inside. There was such a lot to tell Mrs. Doughty! All about Phoebe and Jammy . . . and about Elijah, too.

# Chapter 10

THE RAIN HAD stopped during the night, and now a watery
sunshine glistened over the wet rooftops. A few houses had
their windows open. In one open casement hung a yellow
canary in a small cage. From another window came the delicious aroma of baking bread—a fragrance powerful enough
to overcome momentarily the smell of the street.

Charlotte walked carefully, for she had Noah in her arms,
on her way to Mrs. Perkins' home for his morning feeding.
He was wide-awake, his eyes intent upon her face. He had
been fretful before they left Mrs. Doughty's house, but now
she felt his body relax. He likes me, she thought, or maybe
he expects that when I take him for a walk, a breast full of
milk awaits him.

Elijah was on her mind, as he had been ever since she woke that morning. She had known that the army might send him down south, but that could mean anywhere from Virginia to East Florida. Yesterday it had been such a surprise, such a pleasant surprise, to find him in Charleston. But her pleasure had quickly turned to concern. What could it be that troubled him so much?

She remembered his visit in November to the little cabin she and Papa had built on Carleton Island. That visit, too, had been a surprise. He had survived the defeat of the Loyalist army at Kings Mountain in October. After being taken prisoner, he had escaped. But instead of reporting to Charleston Headquarters, he had travelled five times that distance to Fort Haldimand, offering the feeble explanation that he felt he should report to the same place he had enlisted in the first place, three years earlier. It made no sense.

She had noticed a change in him even then. He had lost all desire to fight, muttering about the stupidity of men dying for a cause already lost.

While she pondered this, she heard his voice calling from behind her.

"Charlotte, wait for me!"

Turning around, she saw Elijah running to catch up.

He overtook her, a little out of breath. "I know it's not yet noon. But the morning drill is finished, and I have two hours free. Your landlady told me which way you were going."

"I'm taking the baby for his morning feeding."

Elijah leaned over to look at Noah. "So that's the baby. He's very small."

"He's only one month old. And I don't reckon he'll grow fast on two feedings a day."

Noah's lower lip quivered.

"We must keep walking," said Charlotte. "If we dawdle, he'll start to cry."

"I thought you and I could talk."

"We can. While he's with the wet nurse."

Elijah fell into step beside her. "This part of town hasn't been damaged at all," he said. "It was lucky to be out of reach of the heavy guns. We caused terrible destruction to some other areas of Charleston."

"We? Were you at the siege?"

"All forty-two days. I'll never forget it." He was silent for a moment. "We had the rebel army trapped inside the walls, and we threw everything at them: grapeshot, musket fire, bombs, red-hot cannon balls."

"It must have been horrible for the people living here."

"When you're a soldier, you don't allow yourself to think about that. We firebombed houses. It's hard to ignore the result when you're close enough to hear children screaming."

Elijah was talking faster and faster, as if he had a demon inside his head that had to come out.

"Near the end, the defenders were shooting back at us with pieces of iron, broken bottles, old axe heads—anything they could jam into a cannon. On May 12, they surrendered. I remember walking around the burnt houses. People came out from cellars where they'd been hiding. Most hadn't eaten for days. Packs of wild dogs were roaming the streets. We had orders to destroy them. Charlotte, I didn't join the army so I could burn cities and kill dogs."

She kept her head down while she listened. She had the feeling that he had barely begun, that worse was yet to come.

"We'd stored the rebels' captured arms in a magazine right in town. A few days later, someone accidentally discharged a rifle. The magazine blew up. Two hundred people died in the explosion—more than were killed during the whole siege.

"I can tell you that when my regiment was assigned to the left flank of Cornwallis's army, I was mighty glad to leave Charleston and go off to fight the Over Mountain men."

They reached Mrs. Perkins' house. Elijah waited in the street while Charlotte took the baby inside. When she rejoined him, he looked glummer than ever.

"Mrs. Perkins says she'll keep the baby for an hour. That will give us time to talk. Where shall we go?" She looked around. The street was full of wagons, horses and pedestrians. "There must be someplace quiet."

"St. Michael's Church."

"We'd disturb people who go there to pray."

"I meant the burial ground. It's quiet, and we wouldn't disturb the folks resting there."

"I reckon not. They're beyond caring."

A few minutes' walk brought them to the corner of Meeting Street and Broad Street. Elijah unlatched the iron gate to St. Michael's burial ground. Within the brick walls, stone and wooden markers were ranged in rows. Charlotte and Elijah stopped beside a gravestone whose incised letters told them that Eleazor Thomas, his wife Matilda and their eight children were now released from the cares of this world.

Elijah stood with one hand on the gravestone, regarding her from under the brim of his forage cap. The whites of his eyes were veined with red. He didn't sleep last night, she thought. There was a nick on his chin, showing that he had recently shaved, and it reminded her that he was no longer a boy, but a young man sixteen years old.

On their families' long trek north from the Mohawk Valley to Carleton Island, Elijah had been a partial replacement for the brothers she had lost. Like them, he became a soldier; at thirteen he put on the uniform of the Royal Greens.

She spoke softly. "What is the problem, Elijah?"

He kept his eyes on hers. "It began with our defeat at the Battle of Kings Mountain." He spoke firmly, as if he had rehearsed what he planned to say. "That's when I realized that we were bound to lose the war. The more I thought about it, the more I questioned why more men should throw away their lives. I went north to Carleton Island, hoping the army would keep me there as a member of the Fort Haldimand garrison. I thought that if I could just wait out the rest of the war, everything would be fine.

"But they sent me back down south. I've been in Charleston a month, and in three days my regiment is off to the backcountry to defend Fort Ninety-Six. But I can't do it. I've had enough."

"You're a soldier. You've been in battle before."

He did not seem to hear her.

"There was one other man in barracks, Sergeant Malcolm, who felt the same way I did. We didn't talk much, he being higher in rank. Even if we'd been equal, there are things soldiers don't talk about. He was a sharpshooter, too. One day he said to me, 'At the beginning of the war, I saw a target whenever I took aim. Now I see a man.' The day after he told me that, he deserted. They captured him heading west into Cherokee country and brought him back.

"After the court martial, we blindfolded him and made him drop to his knees. Then we shot him. We shot him four times before he was dead." Elijah looked away. "I'd rather be shot myself than take part in another execution."

"What can you do?"

"The same as Sergeant Malcolm did. Just hope for a better outcome. I know a place to hide, an abandoned cabin. I found it by accident while reconnoitring before the siege. It's in the swamp about ten miles northwest of Charleston."

"Whoever would be so foolish as to build a cabin in a swamp?"

"A newcomer who knew no better. In summer, the flood plain is solid ground. It would look like a good place to clear land for a farm. The settler couldn't have known what happens in late winter, when the creeks overflow their banks. When I saw the cabin—that was in April—it was a foot deep in black water. But there's a loft you can reach by a ladder. That's where I plan to hide. The fighting can't last much longer. General Cornwallis will have to give up."

"Elijah, what makes you think nobody will look for you there?"

"I doubt anyone knows about the cabin. It's hidden by trees. From the look of the place, nobody's been there for years. The swamp is crawling with alligators."

"You say it's just ten miles from Charleston. Wouldn't you be safer farther away?"

"Southern Command has better things to do than send a platoon to search for one runaway private. If the war ends soon, there be no more need to hide. If it doesn't, I'll move on."

"How will you live while you wait?"

"I'll stuff my cartridge cases with hardtack biscuits. In the swamp, I can set snares. On the ridges there are deer and turkeys. I'll have plenty of time to fashion a bow and some arrows."

"I'll never forget how you learned to hunt with a bow and arrow."

"Nor shall I."

"It was after we left the Mohawk Valley, when we were camped beside Oneida Lake. I was watching when that young warrior, Okwaho, tied a dead squirrel high up in a pine tree. He made you shoot and shoot until finally you hit it."

"And then he took me deer hunting." Elijah smiled. "I haven't used a bow and arrow for three years. I reckon I still can . . . after a bit of practice."

"When will you leave?" Charlotte asked.

"Tonight."

"That soon?" She saw that there was no way she could dissuade him. All he had needed from her was a listening ear. "People who care about you should be able to find you."

"Who cares about me?"

She laid her hand upon his arm. "I do. You and I have been friends for a long time."

"Through thick and thin." He nodded. "All right. I'll tell you as best I can. Follow the broad way north out of Charleston. The first three roads branch to the left, then there's one to the right. That's the road to take. It skirts the swamp. There are plenty of trails leading in. I can't be clearer than that."

She withdrew her hand. "Unless there's an urgent reason, I won't tell a soul."

They left the graveyard together. He went into the church instead of walking back along Meeting Street with her.

A long, hard road lies ahead for him, she thought. Who knows what he'll find at the end?

# Chapter 11

AS THE DAY WORE ON, a feeling of dread settled over Charlotte. She feared for Elijah's safety, because it seemed likely that if soldiers on his own side did not capture him, then the rebels would. She feared for him in other ways as well. Even if he reached the abandoned cabin, an alligator-infested swamp was not a good place to spend months alone in hiding. In such a situation, his melancholy might deepen to despair.

Her fears for Elijah spread like a contagion. For three years she had tried not to worry about Nick, telling herself over and over how resourceful he was, how skilled in the wilderness, how clever at avoiding capture. But by the end of that one day, her powers of self-persuasion had drained away.

That night, lying on her cot in the kitchen, she fretted and stewed, counting the days until the end of February, struggling to remember the exact words of Nick's letter. She could expect him *before* the end of February, couldn't she? How much before?

Maybe Mrs. Knightly had news of him. Perhaps there was even a letter from Nick waiting for her at the officers' quarters. Charlotte had been in Charleston for nearly a week. It was time to find out. She would do it tomorrow. In between picking up the day's load of dirty clothes and taking Noah for his second feeding, there would be enough time.

Having made up her mind, she was at last able to sleep.

The next afternoon she took her new gown and bonnet and a white lawn kerchief from her trunk. It was fine for an old friend like Elijah to see her wearing shabby old clothes, but for a visit to the officers' quarters she must look like a lady. She dressed carefully, knotting the kerchief on her bosom. Finally she put on the handsome blue cloak that she had bought in Quebec before embarking for Charleston.

There was no looking glass in the house, for Mrs. Doughty would never have owned such an aid to vanity. But Charlotte knew that this afternoon no one would think she was the poor white helper of a washerwoman.

When she arrived at the officers' quarters, Mrs. Knightly greeted her with smiles and the tiniest dip of a curtsey, which Charlotte returned.

Today Mrs. Knightly wore green silk, and a cap trimmed with fine lace. "Well, I declare!" she said. "You're just in time for afternoon tea."

She and Charlotte sat down on the upholstered settee in the common room and waited for a slave to bring their refreshments.

"I hoped there might be news about Nick," Charlotte began.

"Alas. There's nothing about him or from him. But I'm so glad you dropped by. I've been worried about you ever since Posy told me that a cutpurse robbed you of your pocket. Why, that's terrible! Was there much money in it?"

"Every penny I owned."

"I ought to have done something to help you, but lately I've been so terribly busy." As she raised her hand to her brow, the emerald on her slender finger flashed green fire. "To think what a pickle my husband has landed you in!"

"Colonel Knightly can hardly be blamed for the loss of my pocket."

"Oh, but I've heard what happened after that. My husband should not have sent you to lodge with somebody who keeps a cellar full of escaped slaves. Everybody's talking about it. I declare, from now on you won't find many of us offering that Quaker woman a helping hand."

"She's a good person," Charlotte said firmly, "and now she has the slave girl's baby as well as her own children to support."

"Well, she ought to send that baby right back to the people who own him."

"They don't want him." Charlotte wondered if Mrs. Knightly was aware of who the baby's father was, but decided not to pursue that subject.

At that moment, the tea arrived, borne on a silver tray by a black woman. Charlotte wondered what she thought of this conversation, for she must have heard the last few words. Her expression revealed nothing.

The nut bread was delicious, and the little iced cakes were the sweetest Charlotte had tasted in a long time. She felt uncomfortable to be waited on by a slave—but not uncomfortable enough to turn down a second slice of nut bread and another cake.

Mrs. Knightly had no news about the progress of the war. It was her practice, she said, to ignore military matters. At the moment, she was busy organizing a ball. The best of Charleston society would be invited. If some of her guests were rebel sympathizers, she was prepared to look the other way.

Charlotte's attention wandered while Mrs. Knightly was describing her new ball gown. As soon as they had finished their tea, she politely took her leave.

"Do drop in any time." Mrs. Knightly clasped Charlotte's hand as she bade her goodbye. "Who knows when a message might arrive from the backcountry?"

"Thank you. I shall."

Maybe next week there'd be a message, Charlotte thought as she stepped outside into the fresh breeze blowing from the harbour. She felt as if she had made an escape. Although Mrs. Knightly had been most cordial, Charlotte was not at ease in the elegant surroundings of the officers' quarters. Thinking it over, she wasn't sorry that Nick's room had been reassigned to someone else. Despite its drabness, she preferred the simplicity of Mrs. Doughty's modest home.

She walked down the brick pathway to the gate and had just put her hand upon the latch, when through the wrought-iron grille she saw a hand reach for the latch on the street side. It was a large hand with bony knuckles. It was a masculine hand that she knew very well.

Charlotte raised her eyes, and there stood Nick. He was smiling at her through the gate. He took off his tricorn hat, and his fair hair shone like gold in the afternoon sun.

For a moment she stood blinking in a dazed sort of way, too astonished to utter a word. Letting go of the latch, she took a few steps back to let him swing the gate open and come through.

"I'm back." Restoring his hat to his head, he held out his arms.

"I didn't expect . . ." she babbled.

"Aren't you glad to see me?"

Then joy beyond expression welled up within her. They hugged and kissed and hugged some more. Leaning into him, she felt his heart beating. Then he released her and held her by the shoulders, beaming at her as if she were the most beautiful girl in the world. At that moment, she knew she was.

She wanted to say, "I love you." But her throat closed up. She felt tears well in her eyes. Then, as if a dam had burst, the tears flowed, rolling down her cheeks. But though she was crying, she was laughing too, and suddenly floating in a warm cloud of happiness.

At that moment the bells of St. Michael's Church began to chime most joyously. And though she knew that they were merely announcing that it was four o'clock, she felt in her heart that they were ringing for her and Nick.

# Chapter 12

"I RETURNED ONLY an hour ago," Nick said after the sound of the bells had faded. "As soon as I'd made my report to Headquarters, I hastened here." His arm was about her shoulders as he steered her toward the door, clearly intending to take her back into the house she had just left. "For weeks I worried about you, thinking of your ship arriving and you finding me gone. But I've just been talking with Ralph Braemar, and he assures me that he met you, brought you here, and delivered my letter."

"He did. Captain Braemar was a great help."

"And you've made yourself at home. God be thanked that you found a warm welcome."

She stopped, turned to face him.

"Nick, I'm not living here."

"You don't live here?" His face looked blank.

"After you left for the backcountry, they gave your room to somebody else and put your things in storage."

"But Ralph told me . . ."

"He doesn't know."

"Where do you live?"

"I lodge with the widow Doughty, in Stoll's Alley. And I have to go there right now."

The bells that had rung so joyously only a minute earlier also reminded her that it would soon be time for Noah's feeding.

Nick showed no sign of moving from where he stood.

"Mrs. Doughty? I know her. I went to Quaker meetings a few times."

"She told me. But now I really must go back. I can tell you everything on our way."

"What's the hurry?"

"I have to take a baby to his wet nurse."

"You *what*?"

"I'm not the only homeless person Mrs. Doughty has taken in. When I arrived, she was already hiding a runaway slave girl with a baby."

"It sounds as though she's carrying on her husband's work."

"Those were the very words she used when I first came to

her home. 'I carry on my husband's work,' she said. I didn't know then what she meant."

"Brave woman—after what happened to him."

"She doesn't seem to worry about danger. Putting food on the table is her main concern. She takes in laundry, and I do the fetching and carrying for her. It's also my task to take the baby to his wet nurse twice a day."

"Can't his mother provide milk for him?"

Charlotte shook her head. "She's gone. Slave catchers caught her but left the baby."

"A great deal seems to have happened," Nick said, "since I left."

Charlotte placed her hand in the crook of his arm, and they set off.

They found Mrs. Doughty sitting in the front room with the baby on her lap. Patience, Charity and Joseph were playing on the rag rug with painted wooden animals: a pig, a cow, a horse.

Mrs. Doughty gave a gasp when she saw Nick, and then she smiled. "I prayed for thy safe return, but did not expect so quick an answer to my prayers."

"Nor did I expect to return so soon."

Charlotte sat down on the wooden settle, where Nick joined her. He took his seat awkwardly, his big frame seeming too large for the small room. Patience and Charity stopped playing and stared at him. Joseph crept to Mrs. Doughty's side and leaned against her knee.

"Thank you for your prayers," Nick said, "and for taking Charlotte into your home. Now I must beg you to make room for me while I try to find lodgings where we can be together."

"Thee is welcome here for as long as thee remains in Charleston, for I doubt thee can find any other place to lodge."

"I know that all too well. Before I was sent to the back-country, my work was to help Loyalist refugees. The Civilian Department tries to find shelter for the homeless—the sort of help that the Society of Friends provides for its members . . . and for others." He paused, looking at the baby.

Noah whimpered.

"He's hungry," said Charlotte.

"I found him a wet nurse," said Mrs. Doughty, "but he isn't getting enough milk."

The whimper became a wail. Noah's tiny fist waved in the air.

"He's trying to put his fingers in his mouth," Charlotte said. "He does that when he's desperate." She stood up and lifted the baby from Mrs. Doughty's lap. "I'll take him to Friend Perkins now."

"I'll go with you," said Nick.

Noah gave a mighty howl.

"His lungs are big enough," Nick observed.

"He'll stop crying as soon as we're walking," said Charlotte. "Whenever I take him outside, he knows he'll soon be fed."

As Charlotte promised, Noah's crying ceased almost as soon as they were out the door. "He needs his mother," Charlotte said. "But I don't think he'll ever see her again."

"How did Mrs. Doughty happen to take them in? Was it something the Quakers arranged?"

"No. The girl—her name is Phoebe—lived with the Doughtys for eight months a couple of years ago."

"She must be the girl that Mrs. Doughty taught to read and write."

"The very same. She belongs to Lewis Morley. He's the baby's father." Charlotte kept her voice very matter-of-fact.

"Ah. One of those situations."

"Phoebe knew that Mrs. Morley wanted the baby out of the house. She decided to escape with him before he was taken from her. She asked her friend Jammy, the stable groom, to help her. They ran away together, with the baby. Jammy hasn't yet been captured. But Phoebe was caught. She's to be sold at next week's slave auction. It's a hopeless situation."

"Not hopeless." He shook his head. "Until the sale is over and the buyer takes her away, something may yet be done."

Nick said nothing more, but he appeared to be deep in thought all the rest of the way to Mrs. Perkins' house.

He waited outside while Charlotte took the baby to Mrs. Perkins.

She returned smiling. "Mrs. Perkins will keep Noah for an hour so we can go for a walk."

Nick drew her hand warmly into the crook of his elbow. "Where shall we go?"

"It doesn't matter. King Street, maybe."

It was a beautiful day. The late afternoon sun bathed the houses in a mellow light. The roadway was not as mucky as usual. They passed a coffee house, from which came the sound of cheerful voices. In one house someone was playing a clavichord, and the music drifting through the open window made her think of home.

"Do you remember how my mother used to play the clavichord?" Charlotte asked.

"I remember. She played beautifully. And so did you."

"Not nearly so well."

"You will someday, when you have a clavichord of your own, and time to practise." He gave her arm a squeeze.

After supper, when Mrs. Doughty had put her children to bed and the baby was asleep in his cradle in the kitchen, Nick, Charlotte and Mrs. Doughty sat together in the front room. Nick seemed unusually quiet, although there was plenty to talk about.

After a particularly long silence, during which he crossed his legs and then uncrossed them, he said, "I've been thinking." He turned to Mrs. Doughty. "You and your husband bought a slave and set him free." Nick spoke slowly and deliberately. Charlotte could tell that he was weighing every word. "If Phoebe were free, could she and the baby have a home with you?"

With a sigh and a shake of her head, Mrs. Doughty answered, "I'd gladly give them a home. But I have no money to buy her. Since Caleb died, no manner of scrimping and saving would make it possible. I would if I could."

"What would it cost?"

"Far too much."

"How much?"

"I don't know exactly. Phoebe is a house servant, trained as a lady's maid. That increases her value. But some people wouldn't want to buy a slave who'd tried to run away. That lowers her value. Twenty pounds might be enough."

Nick answered vaguely, "Then there'd be the lawyer's fee to draw up the document of manumission."

Charlotte saw the light in his eyes that gave a glow to his whole face whenever he was excited. She knew what he was thinking.

"I've just received my quarterly pay. Twenty-five pounds."

Mrs. Doughty's eyes shone from the shadow of her poke bonnet with brightness that equalled Nick's.

Nick turned to Charlotte. "What do you think?"

Charlotte gulped. If they bought Phoebe, there would be no money left to rent a place for the two of them to live . . . though they probably couldn't find one anyway.

And then she felt like shaking a finger at herself. How could she, even for an instant, be so mean as to place her own comfort ahead of something so important!

She smiled. "It's a wonderful idea."

"Tomorrow I'll find out details about the sale," said Nick. "There's sure to be a poster put up near the Exchange."

"There's going to be an advertisement in the *Royal Gazette*." Charlotte felt good about herself again. "I heard a couple of gentlemen talking about it in front of a coffee house."

Mrs. Doughty went into the kitchen to close the shutters there. She returned with a lit candle in a candlestick. "Here's a bit of extravagance to celebrate Nick's safe return."

That night, two straw-filled mattresses lay side by side on the rag rug covering the trap door. At last Charlotte was able to wear for Nick the almost perfect nightgown she had bought in Quebec.

It's not a dream, she said to herself with happiness so great she could hardly believe it. We're together at last. We'll never be parted again.

# Chapter 13

LOUD SINGING WOKE Charlotte and Nick in the middle of
the night:

> I am a man upon the land,
> I am a silkie in the sea.

It sounded like two men, both very drunk:

> And when I'm far and far from land
> My home it is in Sule Skerrie.

What on earth was going on! The singing stopped. Then
the banging and thumping on the door began. Charlotte was

thankful that Mrs. Doughty no longer left doors unlocked.

"Not that house, laddie," a slurred voice said. "We're on the wrong street."

"Noo, why dinna ye tell me?"

Another burst of fists hammered on the door.

"I did, but ye wouldna listen. 'Tis too late anyway. Let's go back to the ship or we'll na escape flogging."

Their voices receded as they moved off, mournfully moaning another verse of their song:

> It shall come to pass on a summer's day
> When the sun shines hot on every stane
> That I shall take my little young son . . .

The sound made Charlotte think of sick wolves howling.

"Lonely Scots far from home," said Nick, "and looking for solace in a tavern."

"They must have taken a wrong turn. There's no tavern in Stoll's Alley."

"As they realize. So now that the entertainment's over, we can go back to sleep."

"Good."

Before they fell asleep, she had a question.

"Nick, what's a silkie?"

"Hm?"

"The song those men were singing: 'I am a man upon the land. I am a silkie in the sea.'"

"A silkie is a seal," he said drowsily. "But not an ordinary seal. A silkie can take off its skin and go on land, just like a man."

"What's the song about?"

"The silkie visits a girl. She doesn't know who or what he is. He leaves her with a bairn when he goes back to the sea. Later, he returns to take the bairn away. He pays her for taking care of his child." Nick sat up, sleep forgotten as he softly sang the song:

> And he had taken a purse of gold
> And he had placed it on her knee.
> "Now give to me my little young son
> And take thee up thy nurse's fee."

"He's heartless," said Charlotte.

"Not really. It's sad for everybody. All Scottish ballads are sad."

The story made her think of Phoebe, separated from her child. But there the similarity ended, for Mr. Morley would never, ever come to take away his son.

"That song's my favourite," said Nick. "But there are hundreds more. Somebody ought to collect them in a book before they're forgotten. In the backcountry I heard ballads from many countries, ballads I'd never heard before. Men sing them in taverns. As a spy, I spent a lot of time in taverns."

"Sneaking around listening to people?"

"No need to sneak. When I came riding into a village on

my handsome bay gelding, everybody gave me a warm welcome. I told them I was the son of a Georgia planter looking for customers to buy my father's cotton. You should have seen me in my embroidered vest and my doeskin breeches. My pouch was stuffed with guineas to buy drinks for the locals. Wherever I travelled, I stayed at the best inn and slept in a feather bed."

There were no feather beds on the *Blossom*, she thought.

"In the evenings I'd buy drinks for everyone, then sit back and listen to people talk. My biggest challenge was remembering to say 'Y'all' and not let my speech slip out of that southern drawl I'd spent weeks practising. No need to ask whether my new friends were Whigs or Tories. Whichever side they supported, words flowed as freely as the beer and rum punch. By the time I'd visited a dozen or so villages, I'd memorized the names of nearly a hundred secret Loyalists who were prepared to keep fighting. There were a lot more villages that I'd intended to visit, but before I'd finished my assignment, I was forced to leave."

"I didn't realize you'd been forced to leave."

"Afraid so. I thought I was a very convincing planter's son. Yet somebody must have seen through me. At the last village I visited, a courier disguised as a traveller passed me a message warning that the Board to Detect Conspiracies had its eye on me." Nick chuckled. "I didn't waste any time. That same night the planter's son disappeared into the hills."

"So that's why you're back in Charleston a month early."

"Yes. That's the reason. Now that I've been recognized, my career as a spy is finished. Someone else will take over from me. And I'll go back to organizing food and shelter for refugees."

"Which side is winning in the backcountry?"

"That's the question. Nathanael Greene is a superb general. Under him, the rebels are taking back South Carolina bit by bit. They're capturing one British outpost after another. But they haven't yet reached Fort Ninety-Six."

"Fort Ninety-Six. You're not the first person to mention that place. Why does it have a number for a name?"

"The reason I heard is that it's ninety-six miles from the nearest Cherokee town. This seems to me a mighty odd reason. But however Ninety-Six got its name, it's not just a fort. There's a village, too, with a courthouse, a jail, a church, a blacksmith, and a tavern."

She smiled. "There's bound to be a tavern."

"True. Having all these things makes it the key to the backcountry. Ninety-Six is where the British forces will make a stand. The fortifications are excellent. Southern Command is confident that Ninety-Six can beat off any attack."

"It sounds as if the rebels are confident, too."

"Very confident. In fact, they already have their own government-in-waiting. Its assembly meets in a village called Jacksonboro, twenty-five miles from here. A committee there is hard at work gathering names of Loyalists. If the rebels win, they'll banish every family on the list and confiscate their property." He hesitated. "Sweetheart, if I'd known how critical the situation was becoming, I wouldn't have asked you to join me here."

"Then I'm glad you didn't know."

The next evening, Nick returned from work with a copy of the *Royal Gazette*. He walked straight into the kitchen, where Charlotte was peeling shrimp and Mrs. Doughty was mixing biscuits. He set the newspaper on the table, the back page up so both of them could read it.

"Two notices," he said. "One for Jammy. One for Phoebe."

The first item he pointed to was set in a box and decorated with a tiny figure of a black man running.

> Run Away from the subscriber, the 20 of January, a Negro fellow named Jammy, age 15, about 5 feet 8 inches high. Black skin with large pits of the small pox on his face. Whoever delivers the said Negro to the workhouse, shall have Twenty Pounds currency reward, and all reasonable charges.
>
> Lewis Morley

Charlotte looked up at Nick. "It says there's a twenty-pound reward. Why would Mr. Morley offer so much money? Jammy's just going to be hanged if he's caught."

"Morley's saying what Jammy's worth. It helps to establish the compensation. When killing a slave is in the public interest, the owner shouldn't be left out of pocket. That's local policy."

"Small justice," she murmured.

"Do you see the advertisement for Phoebe, lower down on the same page?"

"Here it is." She read it aloud:

> To be Sold at Auction in front of the Exchange on February 3. Negro wench named Phoebe. Age 15. 5 feet high. Speaks excellent English. Pleasing manner and appearance. Skilled seamstress. Expert at embroidery and lace making.
>
>                              Thomas Watkins, Auctioneer

"It won't be a big auction," said Nick, "not like the ones they hold when a slave ship arrives from Africa. At those auctions, they put hundreds of slaves on the block. Plantation owners come from all over the South to buy them. The sale tomorrow will just be a domestic auction."

"Domestic?"

"The slaves offered aren't new stock from Africa. Most were born right here in the Carolinas. They're already somebody's property. Some are skilled artisans: carpenters, tailors, dressmakers. They're worth a great deal of money."

"The advertisement doesn't mention that Phoebe can read and write."

"Of course not. Literacy lowers her value because it marks her as a possible troublemaker."

"That's why there's a law against teaching a slave to read," said Mrs. Doughty. "Slaves who can read get dangerous ideas. They learn about liberty and think, 'Why not me?' The spread of such ideas could bring about the end of slavery."

"Amen," said Charlotte. She folded the newspaper and handed it to Nick. "What sort of person is Mr. Morley?"

"He's a Charleston businessman, an importer."

"Does he have many slaves?"

"Not many," said Nick. "A couple of dozen labourers and household servants. It's not as if he owned a plantation. It's common for rice and indigo growers to own hundreds of field workers."

"But Mr. Morley is a rich man, isn't he?"

"Very rich. He buys merchandise from shipmasters who bring goods from all over the world: England, Scotland, the Netherlands, France, the West Indies, the East Indies. Silks and fine furnishings, tea and coffee, ploughshares, rifles. Morley owns a big warehouse down by the wharves."

"And he's a Loyalist."

"No doubt about that. You'll see him every Sunday with his family in their box at St. Michael's Church, joining his voice in the Prayers for the King."

"Pity."

"What do you mean?"

"If he were a rebel, Jammy could flee behind British lines to gain his freedom. In one year he would be given a General Birch certificate. Captain Braemar told me about that."

"It's true. But Lewis Morley is staunchly on England's side."

# Chapter 14

BACK IN THE Mohawk Valley, Charlotte had gone with her father and brothers to many auctions at the Johnstown sales barn. It had not bothered her to see a farmer pull back a horse's lips to check its teeth or run his hands up and down its legs. But to see these same actions performed on men and women made her ashamed to be white.

She tightened her grip on Nick's arm. "Those people are being treated like livestock."

"They *are* livestock. It makes me sick."

The slaves to be auctioned were separated by sex, lined up in order of height, and chained together with their ankles shackled. The women were to the left of the platform, and the men to the right. There were six women and nine men —a small auction, as Nick had said.

From the list handed to Nick at the door, Charlotte quickly learned which slave was Phoebe.

> Number 3. Wench. Phoebe. Age 15. House servant. Skilled seamstress. Expert at embroidery and lace making.

So this was Noah's mother, the girl whom Mrs. Doughty had taught to read and write. Phoebe must have felt Charlotte staring at her, for she turned and met Charlotte's eyes in a steady gaze. Charlotte looked away, embarrassed to be caught behaving like a prospective buyer previewing the merchandise.

"She's very pretty," Nick said.

"Right now, she likely wishes she weren't. The way men are looking at her, I'm sure it's not lace and embroidery they have in mind."

There were about sixty white people attending the auction. All of them, except two men, were looking at the slaves. Those two men were staring at Nick.

They stood side by side, leaning against one of the pillars of the Exchange. Both wore buckskin jackets, leather breeches, and thick high boots. One had a coonskin cap on his head, and the other a broad-brimmed hat with a flat top. The man with the coonskin cap had an aquiline nose that stood out like a beak beyond his receding chin. The man with the hat had bushy eyebrows and small eyes that squinted when he talked. He was talking now, leaning his head toward his companion as they stared at Nick. The man in the coonskin cap frowned and shook his head.

Charlotte nudged Nick. "Do those fellows know you? They're watching you."

Nick did not turn his head. "I noticed them already. They're Over Mountain men from the backcountry. They likely think they recognize me, but they're not sure. Ignore them. Don't let them see you've noticed them." He took her arm. "Keep your eyes on the stage. The sale is about to begin."

The auctioneer stepped onto the platform. He was a sweaty-faced bald man, wearing a linsey-woolsey shirt with a red neckerchief. A thin young fellow who appeared to be his assistant removed the chain from the ankle ring of the tallest woman and dragged her by the elbow onto the platform. The woman's ebony skin shone as if it had been oiled. With her broad shoulders and muscular arms, she was a picture of health and strength.

"Who'll start the bidding at twenty pounds for this fine field worker? She knows rice growing like the back of her hand. Never been sick a day in her life. Thirty years old and in her prime. Let's hear twenty pounds."

"Fifteen!" a man shouted.

The bidding went up quickly, one pound at a time. The new owner paid twenty-five and looked pleased as he led her away.

The next woman brought onto the platform was older, perhaps forty. She had a sinewy look, with knotted muscles, and skin marked by smallpox scars.

"This one don't look so pretty," the auctioneer admitted. "But those pock marks prove she's already had the sickness. So she ain't going to up and die next time there's an epidemic. And look at those broad hips. Good breeding hips. She's had eight children, and never lost a one."

"She's old," a man shouted. "Ready for the knacker!"

Apparently most buyers agreed. This woman went for ten pounds.

Phoebe was next. Slender and only five feet tall, she wore a simple gown of brown homespun. It was a cheap gown, but on Phoebe it did not look cheap. There was a natural grace to her bearing that nothing could diminish—not even the brass collar around her neck. She held her head high. But from the way her eyes blinked, Charlotte suspected that she was close to tears.

Holding Phoebe by both shoulders, the auctioneer's assistant turned her around to display her from all angles. Hoots and whistles made clear that the men present appreciated what they saw.

The auctioneer began, "Now here's a pretty little wench. Not strong enough for heavy work," he snickered, "but she's good for other things. Who'll start the bidding at twenty pounds?"

A man standing next to Charlotte, on the other side from

Nick, gave a wink as he remarked to the man with him, "That's Lewis Morley's slave girl. His wife won't have her in the house."

"I'd be happy to take her off his hands," said his companion. "But if I arrived home with that girl, my wife wouldn't let *me* in the house."

Good! Charlotte thought, grateful for anything that might discourage bidding. If enough husbands were equally afraid of their wives, Phoebe's price might stay low enough for Nick to afford her.

Nick opened the bidding. "Fifteen pounds."

"Sixteen." The voice came from further back in the crowd. Turning to look, Charlotte saw a young man who was leaning forward slightly, an eager look on his face. His ill-fitting dark brown coat looked slightly threadbare, and his white cravat needed to be pressed.

"Seventeen," Nick countered.

The young man hesitated. "Eighteen."

"Nineteen."

Charlotte's eyes did not leave the young man's face. His throat moved. He gulped.

"Do I hear twenty pounds?" the auctioneer's voice boomed.

"Twenty," the young man's voice was a frightened squawk. He can't afford it, Charlotte thought.

"Twenty-one," said Nick.

She heard the confidence in his voice.

"The bid is twenty-one pounds," said the auctioneer. "Do I hear twenty-two?"

He did not.

"Going once at twenty-one pounds." A pause. "Going twice." Another pause. He was giving the young man time to reconsider. "Going three times."

The young man shook his head, defeated.

Nick and Charlotte exchanged a smile. Then Nick stepped up to the platform and offered Phoebe his hand to help her down. Turning her head away, she rejected his courtesy. He had to take her by the arm to lead her toward the table where the auctioneer's clerk was settling business.

The Over Mountain men were watching Nick.

The next slave to be put on the platform was a mulatto woman. She had a baby in her arms and a little boy peeping out from behind her skirts. As the crowd swarmed forward to examine the trio, Charlotte approached the table where Nick stood counting out coins under the watchful eyes of slave market officials.

Nick looked up as Charlotte reached the table.

"Here you are. Good." He handed her a tiny brass key. "This unlocks her collar. Take her to Mrs. Doughty's house. I'll see you there in an hour or two. I have to sign some papers here, and then go to the lawyer's office to give instructions for the deed of manumission."

Phoebe's eyes swept from Nick's face to Charlotte's and back again. Her lips moved, softly repeating the syllables: "man-you-mis-sion." She looked stunned.

She understands, Charlotte thought as she stepped up to her. But it must be hard for her to believe what's happening.

"My name is Charlotte Schyler. That's my husband Nick. We lodge with Mrs. Doughty. When we reach her house, we'll get rid of that collar." She put the key into her pocket, took Phoebe's hand, and led her away. Phoebe said not a word.

When they had walked half a block and the auctioneer's voice no longer reached them, Charlotte stopped. Still holding Phoebe's hand, she said, "Now let me explain."

But before she could, Phoebe said, "Miss Charlotte, I already know about you. Mrs. Doughty came down to the cellar to tell me a young lady, name of Charlotte, would be staying in the house. She said I mustn't let my baby cry. You weren't supposed to know we were there."

"I heard him cry just once, but I had no idea what was going on . . . even when that slave catcher dragged you out the door."

"The slave catchers followed Jammy right into the house. There were two of them. As soon as Jammy had the trap door open, one came right down into the cellar to grab me and drag me out. Jammy got away. I never knew what happened to Noah."

"The slave catchers didn't touch him. Noah's fine. He's still at Mrs. Doughty's house. In ten minutes, you'll be with him again."

But it took only five minutes, because now it was Phoebe leading Charlotte, and she fairly dragged her along.

# Chapter 15

AS SOON AS PHOEBE was inside the door, Patience, Charity and Joseph ran to her and threw their arms around her knees. "Phoebe, Phoebe!" they squealed. With pats and kisses, she embraced all three, but scarcely seemed to see them. A baby's cry came from the kitchen, and in a moment Mrs. Doughty appeared.

She hugged Phoebe. "Noah's just started to fuss. I was preparing sugar water to give him when I heard thee at the door. His cradle's in the kitchen."

Before Phoebe could rush to him, Charlotte caught her arm. "One thing first."

Phoebe stood motionless while Charlotte inserted the

little key into the lock at the back of the metal collar. The clasp opened with a click. Spreading the two halves open on their hinge, Charlotte slipped the collar from Phoebe's neck.

"You'll never have to wear that again."

Phoebe turned around, and they both eyed the thing in Charlotte's hand as if it were a dead viper, its venom spent. Touching her fingers to her neck, Phoebe looked as if she were about to say something. But Noah gave another cry, and she ran from the room.

Charlotte closed the kitchen door, leaving mother and child together.

Facing Mrs. Doughty, Charlotte took a deep breath and let it out with a long sigh. "Everything went as planned. Nick will be back in an hour or two."

"Thanks be to God!" Mrs. Doughty took her cloak from a hook near the door. "I'm going up Meeting Street to thank Friend Perkins and tell her that the baby is with his mother again. I'll be back before Nick returns."

Charlotte sat down on the rug to play with the children. They built a fort with blocks, and then turned it into a farm, bringing out their wooden animals to put in the barnyard.

After a while, Phoebe joined them. "Noah's asleep," she said as she got down on the rug and helped to turn the farm into a castle.

Mrs. Doughty came home. She brought out her mending bag and started darning stockings.

An hour passed.

The children tired of blocks. Charlotte told them the story of Sleeping Beauty, followed by Rapunzel.

Another hour passed. The tall clock in its wooden case chimed six. Having no idea how long it took to give instructions to a lawyer, Charlotte tried not to worry. But surely it was time for Nick to return!

She helped Mrs. Doughty cook supper. When it was ready, she could scarcely eat a bite.

Mrs. Doughty put her children to bed. After closing the shutters, she lit a candle. It was now eight o'clock. The tall floor clock's brass pendulum swung back and forth, catching the candlelight.

He'll come soon, Charlotte thought. The clock kept ticking.

At nine o'clock there was a knock at the door. Charlotte's heart thudded in her chest. It couldn't be Nick. He would have walked right in.

"Shall I go to the door?" Charlotte asked.

Mrs. Doughty nodded.

When Charlotte opened the door, she saw Captain Braemar standing there, not a trace of a smile on his face. He bowed.

"Miss Charlotte, I have bad news."

Her stomach lurched. "For the past couple of hours, I've been fearing bad news." She opened the door wider for him to enter. "Tell me what happened." She spoke carefully, standing rigid as a gatepost.

"Ruffians attacked Nick and carried him off."

She wanted to scream. But that was what she must not do. She must keep her head. Screaming would help no one.

"I can't tell you much more," said Captain Braemar. "I wasn't there. A mutual friend came to tell me what happened. He said half a dozen men followed Nick from the slave market. They grabbed him right after he left the lawyer's office. Then they tied his hands behind his back and marched him north along King Street. That's all I know."

"Where do you think they took him?"

"It depends who they are. I suspect somebody from the backcountry recognized Nick as the planter's son who turned out to be a spy. If I'm right, I think they'll take him to the swamp for questioning. There are bands of rebels operating in the swamp."

"Two men were watching Nick at the slave auction. He said they were Over Mountain men, and he thought they recognized him. Yes. That makes sense."

She didn't need to ask what fate awaited Nick when their questioning was done. Her voice trembled. "What will Southern Command do about it?"

"Nothing. Spies are on their own."

"But Nick serves with Southern Command."

"He's with the Civilian Department. Rules protecting prisoners of war don't apply to him."

He reached out for her hand. But she drew back so that he would not discover how she trembled. "I'm sorry to bring you such bad news." He hesitated. "My regiment has been ordered to the backcountry. I leave in two days to join the defence of Fort Ninety-Six. Before I go, is there anything I can do for you?"

"I don't think so."

"Then I'll take my leave."

He turned away, but before he had taken two steps, she called out, "Just a minute, Captain Braemar. There is something you can do."

"Yes, ma'am?"

"Do you know which lawyer Nick went to?"

"Joshua Ward. I recommended him to Nick. He's our family solicitor."

She kept her voice steady. "When the deed giving Phoebe her freedom has been prepared, will you pick it up for me?"

"I'm not sure he can release it. Nick may have to sign it first. But I'll ask."

"Thank you. You're a true friend to Nick." She bowed. "Captain Braemar, if you're able to obtain the deed of manumission, please give it to Phoebe if I'm not here."

"Do you plan to be away?"

Swallowing hard, she said, "I think I must."

# Chapter 16

AS LONG AS Captain Braemar was present, Charlotte managed to keep up a show of fortitude. But the moment the door closed behind him, she let herself go. One hand covering her face, she groped her way to the settle and dropped. Overcome, she put her head down on her knees and burst into tears.

Mrs. Doughty came to her, sat beside her on the settle, and took her hand. "Poor girl, poor girl!" She stroked Charlotte's hand. "We must pray for Nick. That's all we can do."

Charlotte raised her head. "Why does God allow things like this to happen?"

"These matters are beyond our understanding. When

Caleb was taken from me, I asked why God allowed such wickedness. I was overcome with grief and bitterness. But I knew there would be no peace for me until I accepted that this was part of God's plan."

Phoebe was crying too, crying and mumbling, "It's because of me. This happened because of me."

Charlotte pulled herself together. "No, Phoebe. It's not because of you. You must not blame yourself. This happened because Nick was a spy in the backcountry, and two men at the auction recognized him."

"He would never have gone to that auction except for me," Phoebe said between sobs. "If he hadn't been there, those two men wouldn't have seen him."

"If they hadn't seen him at the auction, they might have seen him someplace else," Charlotte replied.

"We must pray for Nick. That's all we can do," Mrs. Doughty said again.

Mrs. Doughty's words roused Charlotte. She gently withdrew her hand from Mrs. Doughty's, stood up, and began to walk around the room. "I believe in prayer," she said, "but I also believe God helps those who help themselves." Putting her thought into words helped to rally her spirit, but she still spoke more confidently than she felt. "What I mean is, I'm not content to sit and wait for the Lord to bring Nick back to me. I'm going to search for him. You heard Captain Braemar. He thinks those men took him into the swamp."

Mrs. Doughty stared at her from the shadow of her

bonnet's deep brim. "Will thee go into the swamp?"

"Yes." Charlotte wiped the tears from her eyes.

"Miss Charlotte," said Phoebe, "the swamp's full of alligators."

"And desperate men," said Mrs. Doughty. "A woman dare not go there alone."

"Well, I dare." She paused. "I'm sure it is too dangerous for a woman. But I don't intend to go there dressed like a woman. I'll disguise myself as a man."

"Disguise is not just a matter of clothing," said Mrs. Doughty. "The smallest action may give thee away. Thee walks like a woman—"

"I know," Charlotte broke in. "But I've done this before. A couple of years ago, Nick and I travelled through the wilderness from Carleton Island back to the Mohawk Valley to retrieve some valuables hidden on our farm. We pretended to be two brothers. Before we left, he drilled me on how to walk like a boy, how to sit, how to slouch. I can still do it."

Mrs. Doughty lowered her head. She looked as if she were praying, or perhaps thinking deeply. After a minute she looked up.

"Thee is right. To travel as a man is safer. To be safer still, thee must disguise thyself as a Friend."

Charlotte sat up straight. This made sense. Maybe not all slaves knew about the Quakers, but all who did must know they were enemies of slavery. As for white people, both Whigs and Tories generally left Quakers alone.

"I'll need the right clothes."

"I still have some of my husband's clothes. Caleb was not a big man. With a little alteration, they will fit."

"I'm quick with my needle," Phoebe offered.

"Quick enough to have them ready first thing in the morning?" Charlotte asked. "There's no time to lose."

That night Charlotte slept fitfully, reaching out for Nick at wakeful moments and feeling a burst of panic not to find him there.

She was glad when morning came. Throwing off her quilt, she stood up, stretched, and tiptoed into the kitchen, where Phoebe was still asleep on her mattress on the floor, and the baby in his cradle. The clothes were ready, folded on the table.

Carrying them, she tiptoed back into the front room and began to dress. As she pulled on the late Mr. Doughty's breeches, she recalled the first time she had donned men's clothing. She remembered how awkward she had felt wearing breeches. But very soon she had discovered how practical they were for travelling through the wilderness. Much more sensible than a gown. She felt confident about her disguise and comfortable with the prospect of pretending to be a young man.

Sounds of life now came from the kitchen. Noah was crying, and Mrs. Doughty was clattering her pots and pans.

Charlotte joined them. With the Doughty children still

asleep upstairs and Phoebe sitting in a corner nursing her baby, the kitchen was quiet. Charlotte ate a quick breakfast of leftover grits.

"I'm ready to go," she said when she had finished eating.

She stood by the kitchen table while Mrs. Doughty and Phoebe gave her a final inspection. Her hair was pulled back in a pigtail under a wide-brimmed black hat. She wore a short grey coat over a long black vest. Reaching nearly to her knees were leather boots that Mrs. Doughty had water-proofed with a boiled-up paste of beeswax, tallow and tar. A satchel, slung over her shoulder, held bread and cheese, a tarpaulin, a Bible, and twenty shillings that Nick had given her from his pay. It also held a file and a sharp knife, tools that she might need in freeing a prisoner.

Mrs. Doughty nodded approvingly. "All who see thee will take thee for a Friend."

"The vest still doesn't fit right," said Phoebe. "You aren't shaped like a man."

"I should hope not! But if I keep the coat on, nobody will notice."

"Does thee know the way to the swamp?" Mrs. Doughty asked.

"I know that King Street becomes the broad way out of Charleston. If I follow it and take the first road that branches to the right, I'll come to the swamp."

"Beyond Charleston," said Mrs. Doughty, "the main road is known as the wagon track. This is all low country. The tides rise and fall twice a day. When the tide is in, the wagon track is half under water. Between Charleston and the rice plantations lie twelve miles of useless swamp."

"How do people go back and forth from their plantations if the road is half under water half the time?"

"Rich people don't use the road. They have schooners to take them by river. The swamp remains as wild as the day God made it. And sometimes I wonder why he did." Mrs. Doughty shook her head. "It may be a sin to have such thoughts, but . . . does thee know what God did on the third day of Creation?"

"He divided the waters from the dry land."

"Exactly. But when I consider the swamp, it seems to me that God failed to complete his work that day."

"Maybe God wanted to leave some place for alligators to live."

"I do not question the ways of the Lord. But why God created alligators is also beyond my understanding."

Charlotte, knowing almost nothing about alligators, had no opinion on that subject. "There's plenty I don't understand, either. But the sun is up, and it's time to be on my way."

Phoebe looked at Charlotte with an expression that mingled hope and doubt. "Miss Charlotte, Jammy may be hiding in the swamp. If you meet him, he'll help you."

"I'm sure he will. And if I find him, I'll tell him you're safe."

"And that I'm waiting for him."

"I'll tell him that, too."

Phoebe looked ready to throw her arms around her. To save her wondering whether she should, Charlotte took the initiative and wrapped her in a big hug. She embraced Mrs. Doughty, as well, before she left.

She was unlikely to meet Jammy, she thought as she started through the quiet streets. It was Elijah whom she hoped to find, since she had some idea where to look for him. If she found him, she would ask him to help her look for Nick. But she would not count on anyone but herself.

# Chapter 17

THE SUN WAS at her back as she passed through the gap in the hornwork wall that stretched across the peninsula at the town's boundary. There was a change in the air as the brackish smell of swamp water replaced the stench of garbage. Beyond the earthen dike that lay on her left, she saw snowy egrets wading in black-water pools. From vast tracks of marsh grass came the calls of redwing blackbirds wintering in the Carolinas—a sound that made her think of home. No more than twenty feet away, a male bird clung to a tall stock of grass. His shiny black feathers set off his red and yellow shoulder patch, and his head was thrown back as he raised his voice in song.

Charlotte paused to listen and to watch. As she watched, a long, slender snout parted the marsh grass like a comb. She saw dark, scaly skin banded with creamy white, and a pair of yellow, bulbous eyes. A leap. A splash. Jaws gaped and snapped shut. In an instant, the bright singer was no more.

She flinched. Charlotte was not squeamish. Back on the farm, she had dealt death to hundreds of chickens. It was partly the suddenness of the act that shook her, and partly the creature's appearance. It reminded her of a storybook dragon from some twisted fairy tale.

Although her search had barely begun, she already felt alone and powerless, cut off from any refuge from the dangers she had resolved to face.

"I won't fail," she said to herself. "Everything will be all right." She said it again, determined to banish fear. "Everything will be all right." Quickening her pace, she strode straight ahead.

Ruts made by wagon wheels scored the muddy road. The ruts as well as the prints of men's feet and animals' hooves were half filled with water.

She passed by the first road that branched off to the left, then the second, and then the third.

About six miles outside Charleston she came to a road that forked to the right. According to Elijah, this was the one that skirted the swamp. She turned in that direction.

At midday she topped a small rise and sat down at the side of the track to eat a bit of bread and cheese. No alligators here. A breeze wafted over her with the softness of a feather brushing her cheek. Today was the fourth of February, but in South Carolina it felt like spring. If only Nick were with her, they could make a picnic of the bread and cheese.

As she sat eating, she saw a big man coming toward her along the track. As he drew nearer, she saw that he was wearing a homespun shirt, leather breeches and thick high boots. Not a soldier. Not a Quaker. His brown hair was cut in a rough fashion, reaching the lobes of his ears. Perhaps he could tell her something. As he drew near, she put away her bread and cheese and stood up, ready for the test. She must speak like a Quaker. She must sound like a young man.

"I bid thee good day."

"Good morning, lad." The stranger looked friendly.

"Can thee help me? I'm looking for my brother. Yesterday he left town to hunt turkeys in the swamp. We thought he'd be back before dark, but he hasn't come home. My mother sent me to look for him. My brother is tall, with fair hair. Twenty-one years old. Has thee seen anyone like that?"

"I have, but the young fellow was not a Quaker. Yesterday, just before dark, I was walking along this very road when I heard a gang of men coming along behind me. They were cursing in a way *you* would never want to hear, you being a Quaker. Since I was alone and didn't like the sound of them, I stepped off the track and waited behind a tree till they went by. There were five of them, and they had a young fellow with them. His hands were tied behind his back. He was tall and blond and about that age. But he wore a plum-coloured coat."

"A plum-coloured coat? No. He couldn't be one of us. I wonder what those men were doing with him, whoever he was."

"Planning some mischief, no doubt. Either he was a Whig, and Tories caught him. Or he was a Tory, and Whigs caught him."

"That sounds likely."

"I've no use for either. You being a Quaker, I'll speak frankly about that. I can tell you that neither lot is on the side of the angels. Both of them plunder and burn. They ought to get over this fuss about whether they want the King or the Congress to rule them."

"Thee speaks the truth." Charlotte was careful to express correct Quaker views.

"What we need to fear is the enemy without and the enemy within. By which I mean the savages and the slaves. South Carolina won't be safe for settlement until every Creek, Choctaw and Cherokee has been cleared right out. And the other thing we need to do is keep the blacks under control. Without a fear of the lash, they'll rise up and murder us in our beds." He stopped to take a breath. "Being a Quaker, you likely don't agree."

"No. I can't say that I do."

"I don't take it amiss. For all your daft notions, I think

well of Quakers. And I hope you find your brother safe and sound." He scratched his head vigorously, as if to stir up his brains. "About a mile on, you'll come to an inn. You might find somebody there who's seen him."

"I thank thee for thy help."

"You're welcome, though I don't see as I've been any help at all."

Oh, but you have! Charlotte thought as she watched him continue on his way.

Mrs. Doughty had told her that this swamp extended for twelve miles. "Twelve miles of useless swamp." Searching for Nick would be like looking for a needle in a haystack. But at least she now knew she had come to the right place. The description of Nick was accurate, right down to the plum-coloured coat. Had others besides this traveller seen him? Everybody said the swamps were full of men in hiding. She wished a few would emerge for long enough to answer her questions.

As the day wore on, clouds blew in from the west, great dark, angry billows. If a storm was on the way, that inn would be a good place to stop for the night. She hoped she would reach it before the rain began. Although she had a tarpaulin that could serve as a waterproof cape or as a groundsheet, she would like to have a roof over her head and a dry place to sleep. Distantly there was a rumble of thunder.

# Chapter 18

THE INN STOOD on high ground above a rippling stream—
the only clean-looking water that Charlotte had seen since
starting out nine hours earlier.

A wooden sign above the door announced that this was
Hewitt's Inn. It was a frame building, with a low, wide porch
reaching across the front. Two men were lounging on the
porch, drinking from tankards. A wagon, its load covered by
tarpaulins, was parked beside the building. A pair of mules
stood nose-to-tail in a paddock, the twitching of their long
ears the only sign that they were awake.

Before approaching the inn, Charlotte knelt by the stream,
cupped her hands, and drank the cool, fresh water. As she
drank, she felt the eyes of the men watching her, but their

scrutiny did not bother her. Her encounter with the stranger on the wagon track had bolstered her confidence that her disguise and her acting ability would fool anyone.

When she rose, wiping her hands on her breeches, she greeted them.

"Good evening."

"Evenin'," they answered, almost in unison.

As she told the story about her brother hunting turkeys, the men exchanged sideways glances.

"What's he wearin'?" one asked.

"Why, a black hat, like mine. A dark grey coat. Black knitted stockings."

When she had finished speaking, the second man said, "We never seen him."

The other agreed. "No sir. We ain't seen any young fellows come along this way. But y'all can ask inside."

From the covert way they looked at each other, she wasn't sure whether they had seen Nick, or not. If they had, they weren't talking. In these dangerous times, there might be any number of reasons to lie. Neither looked as if he were ready to divulge any further information.

Charlotte had never been in an inn before. Nick spoke well of the experience, but from the outside this small, backwater inn did not strike her as the kind of hostelry likely to provide the weary traveller with a feather bed.

Her heart was thumping as she pressed the latch.

The room she entered had a low ceiling, bare-board walls, and a brick fireplace. She looked around. There was a little light from the fire, and more came through the two windows in the front wall. A door in the back opened onto a kitchen, where a white woman wearing an apron and a mobcap sat at a table peeling shrimp. Against the right wall, a steep staircase ascended to the upper floor. On the opposite side of the room were three long trestle tables, each with one end butting against the left wall.

There were three men in the inn's main room. One of them, a portly fellow who wore a homespun smock over his clothes, stood next to a sturdy frame on which rested three beer kegs. He must be the innkeeper, Charlotte thought.

The other two men were seated side by side, close together at one of the tables. One had a coonskin cap on his head, and the other a wide-brimmed hat with a flat top. When they looked up, her blood ran cold. These were the men who had been watching Nick at the slave auction. There was no mistaking either the beaky nose and receding chin of the one wearing the coonskin, or the bushy brows and squinty eyes of the other.

For a moment, she thought that Bushy Eyebrows recognized her. He squinted at her, but then, with a shrug, broke off his gaze.

She relaxed, reminding herself that in her Quaker garb she looked nothing like the young lady who had been with Nick at the slave auction. If Bushy Eyebrows showed any interest in her, it was probably because a Quaker entering an inn was a rare sight.

Speaking loudly enough for all three to hear, she described

her fictitious brother in his Quaker garb and enquired whether they had seen him.

"Sorry," said the innkeeper, "I can't help you."

"Not many turkeys in this part of the swamp," said Beaky Nose. He had a shrill voice to match his sharp features. "Y'all better go a ways back along the trail and straight ahead. The ground's higher that way. Round here, muskrats and alligators are all anybody's like to find."

A bolt of lightning lit up the room, followed by a deafening crack of thunder. Charlotte flinched. "I'll take thy advice, yet I fear my search must wait until tomorrow." She turned to the innkeeper. "Can thee provide me with a bed for the night?"

"Sixpence. That includes supper and breakfast."

After Charlotte had dug the coins from her satchel, he pointed to the staircase. "Take any bed you like. We're not full tonight. My wife will have supper ready in half an hour."

Charlotte went up the stairs directly into a large room that held six beds. Each bed had a thin mattress on which lay a folded quilt. Off to one side stood an open keg. She quailed. Oh, no! Not a honey bucket! She wrinkled her nose. There had been a honey bucket in the barracks at Fort Haldimand, an uncovered half-barrel for men to relieve themselves if they didn't want to go outside to the latrines in the middle of the night.

I'll pull my quilt over my head, she thought, and not see a thing.

At the top of the stairs, a door stood open, letting her look into a smaller room. This room was furnished with a double bed, a wardrobe, a small table and two chairs. Was this room for wealthy guests? It was certainly more comfortable looking than the other.

But a second glance told her that the smaller room belonged to the innkeeper and his wife, for she saw a woman's bonnet on a hook, a framed sampler on the wall, and a covered chamber pot under the bed.

Turning back to the larger room, Charlotte chose the bed furthest from the honey bucket, took off her boots, and lay down. After her long walk, she needed a rest. Maybe she could nap for half an hour, taking advantage of having the room to herself.

Almost at once she heard raindrops on the roof, followed by a peal of thunder so loud it shook the windowpanes. She pulled the quilt up to her chin, listening to the rain hammer harder and harder.

Her heart was hammering nearly as hard as the rain when she thought of the night to come. Here she was, under the same roof as the two men who had been watching Nick at the slave market. Tonight she would try to eavesdrop on their conversation. With luck, she might discover whether there was a connection between their presence here and Nick's abduction.

Turning her head, she saw through the windowpanes rain sweeping in sheets across the swamp. The sky looked leaden and bruised. Where was Nick? Not outside, she hoped, while the storm raged.

She rested but did not sleep. When she judged that half an hour had passed, she went downstairs. The men who had been lounging on the porch were now indoors. Wood had been added to the fire, so that it blazed more brightly. On the walls, candles burned in tin sconces. The woman who had been peeling shrimp was dishing up the fruits of her labour: grits, shrimp and biscuits.

The innkeeper handed Charlotte a tankard. "You Quakers don't object to a draught of small beer, I hope. It comes with the meal."

"Oh, no. Of course not."

Charlotte had never tasted beer. She had enjoyed wine on special occasions. But decent young women never drank beer. What about Quaker men? She had no idea.

Charlotte supposed that she could ask for water. But since she didn't want to draw extra attention to herself, she lifted the tankard to her lips.

It tasted bitter, but good in its own way. She would drink slowly, she resolved, and not too much. The Quaker principle of moderation would be her guide.

Beaky Nose and Bushy Eyebrows were still sitting side by side at one of the trestle tables, now with food and drink placed in front of them. Carrying her tankard of beer and her plate of food, she sat down at the next table, with her back to them. They were so close that her chair bumped against Beaky Nose's chair until she pulled hers in.

If she acted as if she were minding her own business, they might be careless about what they said. A quiet young

Quaker, absorbed in studying his Bible, would not be suspected of eavesdropping on their conversation.

After finishing her meal, Charlotte took from her satchel the Bible that Mrs. Doughty had given her. It troubled her conscience to use a Bible in such an underhanded way.

"Lord, forgive me," she murmured as she opened it at the place where a bookmark had been inserted between the pages. Psalm 46, she read:

> God is our refuge and strength, a very present help
>     in trouble.
> Therefore will not we fear, though the earth be
>     removed, and though
> the mountains be carried into the midst of the sea:
> Though the water thereof roar and be troubled,
>     though the mountains shake
> with the swelling thereof.

She could hear waters roaring outside the inn. On a night like this, it would be hard to pick a Psalm more in tune with the weather. This part of South Carolina lacked mountains, but the raging creeks were doing their best to carry any bit of land still above water into the midst of the sea.

She read no further. Beaky Nose and Bushy Eyebrows were starting to talk.

"... he was no more a planter's son than a flying pig." That was the shrill voice of the former. "But he sure 'nough had us fooled."

"I never thought to see him again," drawled Bushy Eyebrows, "the way he slipped away in the middle of the night. But there he was a week later, right in the heart of Charleston, bidding on that girl like he really was a planter's son."

"Sure has an eye for pretty women. Did y'all notice the young lady with him?"

"I did indeed." Bushy Eyebrows gave a chuckle. "If my old woman looked like that, I wouldn't need a black girl on the side."

Oh, really! Charlotte thought, her ears burning. Not her Nick! If they think that Nick would ever . . .

Hunched over the Bible, she endured more remarks of a similar nature until the snickering stopped and Beaky Nose and Bushy Eyebrows returned to the subject of the supposed planter's son.

"Now that our friend's had another night chained in the cave, he should be ready to talk," said Beaky Nose.

"He's pretty tough."

"There's nothing like sitting in swamp water to soften a man. If he won't talk tomorrow, we can try fire ants."

"He must know a hundred backcountry names we can add to the list," said Bushy Eyebrows. "Tories. Families supplying food to British soldiers. There'll be mighty good farms for the taking, after the Assembly banishes those traitors and seizes their property."

"Here's to Liberty!" Beaky Nose raised his voice in a toast. "And to Prosperity!"

While their tankards clinked, she kept her eyes on the page. So they had Nick sitting in swamp water, chained in a cave. But where?

Her first idea had been to find Elijah and ask for his help. But it turned out she didn't need Elijah's help. If she could follow these men, they would lead her straight to the cave.

Beaky Nose and Bushy Eyebrows went on to praise a man named Francis Marion, leader of a band of rebels they called swamp dodgers. These fighters, she learned, were busy picking off British outposts and ambushing Loyalist troops on the march to defend Fort Ninety-Six. She also heard a prediction that Charleston would be surrounded by the end of summer. None of this surprised her. It was what Nick expected, too. He had told her, on the night he returned from the backcountry, that the rebels were taking over South Carolina bit by bit.

When the two men left their table, Charlotte waited for a while to give them time to go to bed. Then she closed the Bible and went upstairs. She crawled onto her bed, pulled the quilt over her head, and did her best to ignore her companions' snores, the honey bucket, the howling wind, and the pelting rain.

# Chapter 19

IN THE MORNING it was still raining. The stream from which Charlotte had drunk the previous afternoon had disappeared under the black and swollen flood. The wagon track had vanished beneath a vast lake that was studded with isolated trees. Water reached halfway to the hocks of the two mules standing forlornly in the paddock. Wavelets lapped at the boards of the porch, where Charlotte now stood by herself, looking about.

She was not alone for long. The two men who had been sitting on the porch when she arrived at the inn came outside.

"Don't worry about your brother, lad," said one. "He'll

have found his way to high ground, where he'll have wild turkeys for company, along with deer and rabbits, if he's still minded to do some hunting."

"When will the water go down?"

"It'll start to drain away after the rain stops. Y'all better stay put for a few hours, 'cause you don't know the currents. One false step could carry you away."

While he was talking, his partner waded to the wagon and retrieved harness from under the tarpaulins.

"Surely thee won't leave this soon!" exclaimed Charlotte.

"General Greene is waiting for these supplies. We've done this before. One time on the wagon track, we sloshed through water for six days. We know the way. The mules do, too."

He stepped off the porch, waded to the paddock, and brought out the mules. While the men were hitching them up, the big, placid animals looked as though they had been through this a hundred times. The men climbed onto their seat at the front, and then the wagon started out, heading northeast. Its wheels were halfway to their hubs in black water.

When Charlotte went back inside, she saw Beaky Nose and Bushy Eyebrows seated at one of the tables, eating grits and drinking coffee. She sat down at the next table. In a few seconds the innkeeper's wife set Charlotte's breakfast in front of her.

While she ate, she tried to overhear what Beaky Nose and Bushy Eyebrows were talking about. Nothing much, she soon realized. The business of eating seemed to require their entire attention. Each sat hunched with his arms virtually wrapped around his plate, as if afraid someone would try to steal it.

After breakfast, she wandered back out to the porch. The rain had stopped. In the distance, the wagon pulled by the two mules was still in sight.

Beaky Nose and Bushy Eyebrows joined her a few minutes later.

"The rate it's going, that wagon won't cover five miles today," said Beaky Nose.

"Don't much matter," said Bushy Eyebrows. "Slow and steady wins the war. Whenever they arrive, General Greene can use those supplies." He turned his head toward Charlotte. "What's your opinion of General Greene?"

"My opinion?"

"He's a Quaker, or didn't y'all know? They call him 'The Fighting Quaker.' Fighting goes against your beliefs, don't it?"

"Well . . . er . . . I don't know anything about General Greene." She was starting to sweat, afraid to say something accidentally that would reveal she was not a Quaker.

"Nathanael Greene has more brains in his big toe than Cornwallis has in his whole head."

"Is that so?" Charlotte murmured politely.

"Look what General Cornwallis did. Burned his own supply wagons so his army could travel light. He's got eight thousand hungry Loyalist soldiers scattered in companies all over the backcountry. Hungry men can't fight. Now, General Greene knows that. He knows you have to feed your men if you want a good fighting force." He pointed to the wagon that was making its slow and steady way northwest. "Y'all know what's on that wagon?"

"No."

"Rice and sweet potatoes to feed the Patriots. We have wagons every week taking food to our fighting men. Last week we had a wagon loaded with hams, two wagons loaded with corn, and another carrying rifles and gunpowder. What do you think of that?"

His words sounded like a challenge. Was Bushy Eyebrows trying to goad her into condemning General Greene for his un-Quakerlike behaviour? She was puzzled to know what a *real* Quaker would say in response.

She answered, "It's an excellent idea to send food for your army. Then the soldiers won't have to steal it. I've heard that both sides raid farms, leaving nothing for local people to eat."

"So you ain't gonna criticize General Greene?"

"I'm sure he has his reasons for whatever he does."

"As for that brother of yours," said Bushy Eyebrows, "what's he think about this war?"

"My brother doesn't take sides." Charlotte shifted uncomfortably. "I just hope nothing's happened to him," she said, trying to change the subject.

"He never should have come here if he doesn't know the swamp," said Beaky Nose. "Neither should you, unless you want to be dinner for an alligator. As soon as the water level goes down, you should follow the track right back to Charleston; that's what you ought to do."

Suddenly Bushy Eyebrows gave a shout. "Billy, look who's comin' this way!"

Charlotte looked in the direction he was pointing, and there was a rowboat approaching the inn.

"Good ol' Rufus," said Bushy Eyebrows. "He knew where to find us."

Charlotte stood watching while the boat pulled up beside the porch just as if it were a dock. The man called Rufus had reddish hair and a ruddy complexion.

"Mornin' Billy. Mornin' Abner." He rested on his oars. "I figured I'd find y'all here."

"It was either that or spend the night in the cave," said Bushy Eyebrows. "Me and Billy reckoned Hewitt's Inn would be a darn sight more comfortable."

So Beaky Nose was Billy and Bushy Eyebrows was Abner. Just knowing their names made Charlotte feel a little more in control.

"Where's Robert and Joe?" Billy asked.

"They went on home," said Rufus. "They was worried about their livestock gettin' caught in the flood."

"That's fine," said Abner. "The three of us can do what needs to be done."

"How'd you get along yesterday with our friend?" Rufus asked.

"No results yet. He's mighty tough," Abner replied as he clambered into the boat.

"We reckon one more night in the cave will have softened him up," said Billy. "If he won't talk today, we'll try fire ants tomorrow."

Billy climbed into the boat after Abner.

"Feels like she's scraping bottom," Billy said.

"That's all right," Rufus answered. "It's just mud. I can push off."

"Three men is too many," said Billy. "If the water goes down much further, we'll go aground. Then we'll be stuck until the next high tide."

"We're all right," said Rufus. "But we can't waste any time." He leaned into the oars, and off they went.

Charlotte, left alone on the porch, watched the boat pull away. It did not, she noticed, follow the same northeast course as the wagon, but headed due north toward a low, wooded island about half a mile away. The boat disappeared around the eastern end of the island, leaving her uncertain whether it had gone ashore or continued on. At least I know the general direction I must go, she thought as she went inside.

The innkeeper was sweeping the floor with a corn broom while his wife cleared the table.

"Now I'm thy only guest," Charlotte said. "The others went

off in a rowboat, and soon I'll be on my way."

The innkeeper stopped sweeping. "Not so fast. You should never walk through flooded land until you can see blades of grass sticking out of the water. That's how you tell the shallow places. Never take a step where no plants are visible, or like as not you'll step off the edge of an underwater creek bank, and the current will sweep you away."

"How long must I wait here?"

"Now that it's stopped raining, the water will start to go down. Maybe by low tide you'll be able to leave. That'll be a few hours." The innkeeper returned to his sweeping. "You know, running an inn during times like these isn't easy. Everything's political. Even asking a person whether he wants coffee or tea."

"How can that be political?"

"It's been political ever since England put a tax on tea. If you offer a Patriot a cup of tea, he's likely to offer you the back of his hand."

The innkeeper's wife called through the open kitchen door, "You Quakers are lucky. Nobody forces you to take sides. I wish we could be treated like that. All my husband and I want to do is wait it out to see who wins."

"We hope that nobody sets his sights on taking over the inn." The innkeeper leaned on his broom. "It's a good inn, though the land's of no value. Would you believe we have six kinds of snakes in the swamp, three of them poisonous? And then there's the alligators."

"I saw one," said Charlotte. She sat down at the table. "It was about five feet long."

"Just a baby!" said the innkeeper's wife as she set down another plate of grits in front of Charlotte.

"Don't scare the lad." The innkeeper resumed sweeping. "Alligators don't bother us much. Of course, if they're hungry, they can move real fast. For a few yards, an alligator can outrun a deer. It swallows the deer—hair, hoofs and all. Then it doesn't need a meal for weeks. Until it gets hungry again, it just lies there basking in the sun."

"When I meet an alligator, how do I know when it ate its last meal? It isn't as if I could ask."

"Look for the bulge," he answered. "A big bulge in the middle means the gator's digesting something big."

"I'll remember that." Charlotte finished her grits, stood up and pushed back her chair. "I noticed an island about half a mile to the north. The men who went off in the rowboat headed in that direction. I think that's where I'll look for my brother."

"Island? That's no island. It's the top of a hill, as you'll see when the water goes down."

Feeble sunshine was now coming through the windows.

"I'll wait on the porch," Charlotte said, "to let thee get on with thy work. But first, will thee sell me a flask that I can fill with clean water, when I find some."

"A penny for the flask," said the innkeeper. "The water's free. We always keep on hand a barrelful from the spring. At high tide or whenever there's a flood, we might as well be in the middle of a desert, for all the water that's fit to drink."

She sat on the porch all morning, watching the supposed island grow wider and wider, closer and closer. What had looked like a lake studded with isolated trees gradually transformed into land. When tips of grass finally emerged, she went back inside to pick up the flask. The innkeeper and his wife wished her good luck in her search.

With her first step off the porch, Charlotte discovered that the water was barely past her ankles, but the bottom was so soft that she sank halfway to her boot tops. Thanks to Mrs. Doughty's concoction of beeswax, tallow and tar, not a drop of water penetrated the leather of her boots.

It must be low tide, she thought as the water continued to drop. Before long she was walking not in water but upon soggy land, picking her way around pools that steamed in the afternoon sun. Beside one pool a sixteen-foot alligator lay motionless. The gator had a deeply ridged back, armoured flanks, a muscular tail, and a huge, swollen belly. With a bulge like that, it can't be hungry, she assured herself. But she couldn't help wondering about the unlucky creature being slowly digested inside. A deer? A hog? Either would be about that size. She gripped the handle of her knife as she walked by. When giving it to her, Mrs. Doughty had said that this was the knife her husband had used to cut out leather soles for shoes.

Charlotte knew how to handle a knife. After her brothers

had gone off to war and there had been nobody else to help Papa on the farm, she had learned to slaughter hogs. A grisly business, but she could do it. With a good knife in her hand, she was the equal of any alligator. That's what she told herself.

# Chapter 20

AFTERNOON IN THE swamp. But under the trees it felt like twilight—an eerie, green twilight. The cypresses were hung with moss like torn curtains. Vines thick as tree trunks grew from tree to tree. Little animals skittered under the brush.

Charlotte hoped she was walking in the right direction. With the dense canopy hiding the sun, it was hard to be certain that she was heading north, the direction the boat had gone. But where was the boat? Where were Rufus, Billy and Abner? Where was the cave?

Maybe this was a wild goose chase and she might as well give up. But she couldn't give up, knowing what fate awaited Nick unless she rescued him. At least she was following a path, she thought. A path always leads somewhere. There's no such thing as a path to nowhere. And since this one seemed to lead in the right direction, she would follow wherever it took her and hope for the best.

A yellow snake with black stripes undulated across the path. It was a very long snake—seven feet at least—and she waited for it to complete its crossing. As the snake finally disappeared into the undergrowth, her eye caught a fleeting movement between the trees, an indistinct figure too upright to be an animal. A rustle of leaves made her ears prick. She fought down panic. To run would serve no purpose. Better to maintain a steady pace and keep a good grip on her knife.

From the prickling in the back of her neck she sensed more than saw that someone was shadowing her, moving at her speed while taking care to remain concealed. It isn't a robber, she told herself, because a robber would have no reason to delay. A robber could leap out to attack her any time he felt like it. So the person shadowing her must have a different motive.

They kept on like this for half a mile before the idea came into her mind that she might not be the only one afraid. Perhaps the unseen person wanted to talk to her but lacked the courage to bring matters to a head. In that case, it was up to her.

And so she stopped, faced the tangled mass of green growth, and said, "Who is thee?"

Silence.

"I know somebody's in there. Thee has no need to hide from me."

The leaves parted. A face peered out. Charlotte saw black skin pitted with smallpox scars, a pair of wide-set dark eyes, and a tangled mop of black hair.

"Jammy?"

The face disappeared into the foliage.

"Please come out. If thee is Jammy, Phoebe has told me all about thee."

A boy emerged as if stepping through a green wall. He was thin and wiry, about the same height as Charlotte. He wore no shoes or shirt. His breeches were torn. Insect bites covered his exposed skin.

"Who are you?" the boy asked. "How come you know Phoebe?"

"I'm Charlotte Schyler."

"Charlotte's a girl's name."

"Yes." As she pulled off her hat, a curly lock of her hair fell loose and bounced gently on her forehead.

He looked at her more closely. "Saints alive! You *are* a girl!" He paused. "Ain't you the girl I seen going into Miz Doughty's house?"

"That's where I live. I was there the night the slave catchers came."

"They caught Phoebe, didn't they?"

"Yes."

"What's gonna happen to her now?"

"She's free. I'll tell you about it. It's good news . . . at least it's good about Phoebe."

As Charlotte's words poured forth, she forgot about "plain speech" and dropped all pretence of being a Quaker. She told Jammy how Nick had bought Phoebe in order to set her free, and how ruffians had seized him and carried him off.

When she came to the end, he said, "So Phoebe's free and they're together—Phoebe and the baby."

"At Mrs. Doughty's house, but not hiding in the cellar."

"And you think your man is somewhere in this swamp?"

"I'm sure of it. At the inn where I slept last night I recognized two men who'd been watching Nick at the slave auction. I heard them talking about a prisoner they had chained in a cave. From the things they said, I knew it was Nick."

"There's a cave not far from here. White folks lived there for a spell. After they left, I was thinkin' of using it myself. Then I saw some different white men go in there."

"What did they look like?"

"Like white men. There were two of them. One was wearin' a coonskin hat and the other—"

"Yes! Those are the men. Did you see them today?"

"No. Yesterday."

Suddenly Jammy lifted his head like a startled deer sniffing the breeze. "Somebody's comin'!" Grabbing her arm, he pulled her off the path and into the tangle of vines and trees. "Get down!"

She threw herself onto the ground. Looking out through

the leaves, she saw too late that she had dropped her hat—the black, wide-brimmed Quaker hat—that she had been holding in her hand. It lay in the middle of the path.

At that moment, Billy and Abner came walking along the trail. Charlotte held her breath.

It took only a moment for Billy to spot the hat and pick it up. "Well!" he said. "What have we here?"

"It's the hat that young Quaker was wearing," said Abner. "All Quakers wear the same kind."

"That's a fact. But you don't see many Quakers in the swamp."

Billy examined the hat. "Could belong to his brother. He said his brother was huntin' here." He paused. "Abner, there's something fishy about this."

Both studied the hat.

"You're right," said Abner. "I smell a rat. What kind of a man lets his hat fall off and don't bother to bend over to pick it up?"

"A man in a big hurry. Maybe something was chasing him. That would explain it. I'm gonna shove the hat in my pack. Maybe we'll meet the owner later on. We can ask a few questions when we give him back his hat."

"If he's that young Quaker," said Abner, "I hope he hasn't stumbled on to the cave. He might do that, lookin' for his brother."

"If he's at the cave," said Billy, "we'll have to deal with him too."

"We'll cross that bridge when we come to it," said Abner. "Let's get moving. The day's nearly done."

"We would've been there four hours ago," Billy grumbled, "if the boat hadn't gone aground. Four hours wasted towing it through the marsh! I said three men was too many."

"Never mind. We'll pay our visit, then get back to Rufus and the boat."

Charlotte and Jammy, both lying flat on their stomach, exchanged a glance.

When the men were out of earshot, she said, "Those are the two men I was talking about, the ones holding Nick. Rufus is the man who carried them away in a rowboat. I wonder where he is now?"

"The water's gone down too much to reach the cave by boat. Most likely they left it by a creek or inlet where the water's deeper. And that Rufus fellow is stayin' with the boat."

"How far is it to the cave."

"'Bout one mile further 'long this path."

"It would be safer for us to take a different path."

"There ain't no other path to the cave." He paused to scratch a mosquito bite. "If you don't mind gators, we can go through the bog."

Charlotte *did* mind gators, but she saw no alternative.

"Can we reach the cave before dark?"

"I figure we can."

"Let's go."

Jammy led her down a slope into the swampiest kind of swamp. With every step, her boots sank into the muck, and she lifted her foot with a squelchy, slurping sound.

They sloshed on without speaking. The air was full of flying insects. Slapping and sweating, they trudged along. It felt like hours before they reached firmer ground.

They had just crossed a creek, using the trunk of a fallen cypress tree as a bridge, when Charlotte caught sight of a cabin almost hidden in the trees. It stood in shallow water, a small log cabin with a cedar-shake roof. Saplings crowded close to the walls on all four sides. The stumps of larger, felled trees were sticking out of the water.

Could this be the abandoned cabin Elijah had told her about? If it was, he might be in its loft at this very moment, peering out at them through a chink in the logs.

She stopped in her tracks. "That cabin . . . does anyone use it?"

"I never seen nobody there."

"Can we have a look?"

"If we waste time, we ain't gonna get to the cave before dark." He gave her arm a pull.

He was right. This was no time to stop and explain about Elijah. She gave the cabin one last glance as Jammy led her away.

# Chapter 21

"THERE'S THE CAVE."

Jammy pointed to an outcropping of rock facing them from the far side of a creek. The outcropping ran as a low ridge as far as Charlotte could see. At its base the receding water had left broken branches, uprooted saplings, and masses of waterweed strewn on the muddy bank, everything coated with ooze.

The cave entrance was a cleft in the rock about two feet wide, five feet high, with an overhang projecting above. When the creek was in full flood, the base of the cave must have been under water. It was not under water now. Boot prints in the mud showed that two men had recently gone inside.

Charlotte and Jammy crouched in the brush on their side of the creek. There was still plenty of daylight, though the sun was low in the west.

"Those men are in the cave right now," Charlotte whispered. "I wonder if they'll stay all night."

"Not if a friend with a boat is waitin' for them. They'll want to join him before dark."

"I'll cross the creek," she said, "and crawl up to the cave mouth so I can hear what's happening inside."

She edged her way to the creek bank and scrambled down its muddy side. The water, now tamely within its banks, was neither deep nor fast. Danger lay only in being seen. As quickly as she could, she waded to the other side.

Safe so far! Charlotte crawled to a pile of flotsam a yard from the cave mouth, lay down with her body pressed against the outcropping, and wriggled into the mess of broken branches and soggy waterweed. Finally, she pulled over herself a leafy branch that covered her completely. Wet and muddy, she hoped that she blended right in with the debris.

She strained to listen to the voices coming from within the cave.

"You must have been lonesome, sittin' here all by yourself just waitin' for us to pay you a visit." That was Billy.

Nick made no answer that Charlotte could hear.

"Might as well tell us now," said Abner, "'cause sooner or later you're gonna anyway. You'll save yourself a heap of pain by giving us the names of those Tory traitors before we have to squeeze them out of you."

"Think about it," said Billy. "If you make us come back tomorrow, we'll stake you out on a hill of fire ants. There's a big nest nearby, just over the ridge. Imagine those little devils crawling all over you. Under your clothes, in your ears, up your nose."

"I don't know any names." Nick sounded very tired.

"Yes, you do," said Abner. "You rode all around the back-country talking to people."

"I can tell you nothing."

"We're wasting our time," said Billy. "Let's go join Rufus before it's too dark to find our way back to the boat. We'll have better luck tomorrow."

"You're right. Rufus is waiting."

Their voices came closer. Charlotte held her breath.

"Pleasant dreams," Billy snickered as he left the cave.

"He'll talk," said Abner, following close behind. "Fire ants never fail."

Billy giggled. "By sunset tomorrow, the planter's son will be hanging from a tree, and you and I will be in Jacksonboro with a list of names as long as your arm."

That's what you think, Charlotte said to herself.

She did not let out her breath until she heard them splashing across the creek. When they were out of earshot, she pushed off from her body the mess of debris that had covered her. Rising to her feet, she glanced down at her clothes. Both the grey coat and long black vest were now the same shade of brown muck.

The sun was setting when she beckoned to Jammy—or at least she beckoned in the general direction of where he was hiding.

He rose from the brush, also as muddy as a fresh-pulled turnip, and waded across the creek to join her. "Do you want me to go inside with you?" he asked.

She shook her head. "We need a lookout. I don't think those men will be back tonight, but just in case . . ."

She entered the cave alone.

The stench struck her first. At bottom there was the sour reek of swamp water. Mixed with it was a sickening, sweetish odour of rot and decay. For half a minute she paused, her nose adjusting to the foul air and her eyes to the darkness. She took another step, stooping to keep from bumping her head. When she could see clearly, the sight made her gasp.

There was Nick, sitting slumped and motionless. Around his neck was a metal slave collar. Stretching from the collar to a pin driven into the cave wall was a chain no more than a yard long. Hand bolts cuffed his wrists behind his back. On his ankles were shackles joined by a ten-inch chain. The way his manacles held him, there was no way he could lie down.

He sat facing sideways, and at first did not see her enter the cave. But perhaps he noticed the shadow she cast with the light behind her, for after a moment he turned his head in her direction.

She said, "Nick. It's me. Charlotte."

"Charlotte?" A wheezing sound came from his throat. "Touch me. I want to be sure you're real."

Kneeling beside him, she pressed her cheek to his. "I'm real."

"I didn't think anyone would know where to look for me."

"Captain Braemar came to tell me what happened. He thought you'd been taken into the swamp." She pulled the file from her satchel. "Mrs. Doughty gave me this. She thought I might need it." She rubbed her thumb along the file. "Where shall I start?"

"With the handbolts. But first, give me water if you have any."

She pulled the flask from her satchel and held it to his lips. He drank with great thirsty gulps.

"I have food, too," she said. "Bread and cheese."

"I'm not hungry."

She put away the flask and picked up the file.

The handbolts consisted off two iron cuffs joined by a thick iron bar. The bar was double the thickness of either cuff.

"I'll begin with the cuff on your right wrist," said Charlotte. "Then you'll have one hand completely free."

*Scritch, scritch*, the file rasped.

"Did you come alone?" Nick asked.

"No. By good luck I found Phoebe's friend Jammy. He's been hiding in the swamp, and he knew about the cave."

"Where's he now?"

"Outside. Keeping watch."

As her file ground away at the metal cuff, she told Nick about her night at the inn and how she recognized the two men who had been watching him at the slave auction.

She kept on filing until her fingers cramped. Then she stretched them, pulled them to ease the joints, and started again. A blister formed in the groove between her thumb and index finger. When the blister broke, the raw skin was too sore for her to press as hard as needed.

"I'll ask Jammy to take over," she said.

"How much progress have you made?"

She ran her fingers around the cuff. "It's too dark to see, but I can feel a groove."

When Jammy took over, Charlotte stationed herself outside the cave to keep watch. Her knees drawn up to her chin and her hands wrapped around her shins, she stared into the darkness, listening to the animal sounds from the swamp and to the *scritch, scritch* of the file in the cave behind her.

Jammy was filing twice as fast as she could. Though not very big, he was strong—all sinew and bone. His hands must be hard from his work in the stable.

After a while, when she remembered that she had not eaten since morning, she took the bread and cheese from her satchel. She ate a little, and then went inside to offer some to Nick and Jammy. Jammy stopped work long enough to wolf down his portion. Nick still wanted only water.

He's sick, she thought as she again held her flask to his

mouth. Who wouldn't be, after being tied up in a stinking cave, half the time sitting in cold water?

"I'm nearly through this cuff," said Jammy as he picked up the file again.

"I'm staying in the cave with you," Charlotte said. "We don't need a sentry this late."

A few minutes later Jammy announced, "That's it! His right hand is free. What next?"

Nick raised his hand shakily to the metal slave collar around his neck. "This."

"It would take too long to file through the collar," said Charlotte. "Just cut the chain that attaches it to the wall."

Crouching at Nick's side in the darkness, she took his right hand in hers. "Your skin feels like ice." While Jammy set to work with the file, Charlotte rubbed Nick's hand and his arm.

"You're a ministering angel," he said. "My blood's starting to circulate. As soon as we're out of here, I'll be fine."

Jammy worked all night. After cutting through the chain that attached Nick's neck collar to the wall, he severed the chain that linked his shackles.

At sunrise they emerged from the cave. By the light of dawn Charlotte saw the pallor of Nick's skin and the redness of his eyes. With the collar around his neck, the iron cuff and hand bolts attached to his left wrist, and the shackles on his ankles trailing links of chain, Nick still wore the instruments of his ordeal.

Soon his captors would return. When they found Nick

gone, they would search for him. Only in Charleston could he be safe. But Charleston was ten miles away, and he was too weak to walk that far. Charlotte saw only one solution.

"Jammy, will you take us back to that abandoned cabin so Nick can rest?"

"He can't rest there. The floor's under water."

"I think there's a loft. A friend told me about an abandoned cabin with a loft you can reach by a ladder. If that's the cabin he meant, we can hide in the loft. It will be dry. Can you find that cabin again?"

"Sure thing, Miss Charlotte."

As they started walking, Charlotte did not like the look of the deep prints their feet were making in the mud. But after a time, when they went through a flooded region where they would leave no tracks, she felt safer.

They came upon the cabin suddenly. It was in a little hollow, with trees crowding all around. If there ever had been glass in the single window, it was there no longer. The door was open, hanging by one hinge.

Charlotte stepped inside. The water reached her ankles.

A brick fireplace, its hearth submerged, took up the entire end wall. In size, the cabin was about eight feet by ten. This could have been a snug little home, she thought, if the settler hadn't built it on the floodplain.

Nick looked doubtful. "Is this it?"

"I'm not sure." She looked up. "I expected to see a trap

door that would open to the loft. But this ceiling has boards all the way across."

"I see one feature that's unusual," said Nick.

"What's that?"

"The moulding around the walls, right under the ceiling. Somebody went to a lot of trouble to trim that wood." Faced with a challenge, Nick seemed to come to life. "Maybe the moulding's not for decoration. It may serve as a ledge to support boards that aren't nailed in place. Let's see if we can find a couple."

The ceiling was only a foot above Nick's head. Raising his free hand, he pushed hard at the board directly over him. It didn't move.

"Not that one," he said.

Starting with the boards closest to the door, he worked his way to the other end of the cabin. The second-to-last board lifted when he pushed. The last one did the same.

"There!" he said. "If we shove those two loose boards out of the way, we have our entrance."

"There's no ladder," said Charlotte.

"We don't need a ladder. I'll give you and Jammy a boost up."

"Not me, Mister Nick. I ain't stayin'. No sir! I've been in this godforsaken swamp long enough. I'm on my way to Charleston to say goodbye to Phoebe."

"Say goodbye! Are you going away?" asked Charlotte.

"Now that Phoebe's free, she can make a good life for herself and the baby. But there can't be any place in that life for me. Not in Charleston."

"Where will you go?"

"North. Or maybe west. Someplace slave catchers can't find me."

Charlotte did not try to argue. Jammy was right. He had to leave.

"Jammy, it's too dangerous for you to go to Charleston. Let me give Phoebe a message from you."

"No. Phoebe's my girl. I can't just run off without seeing her one more time."

Charlotte paused, knowing she would feel the same if she had to leave Nick and knew that it might be forever. "Just be careful," she said.

"Phoebe and I have a signal that she'll recognize. If you tell me where she sleeps . . . ?"

"In the kitchen."

"Good. I can creep around to the backyard at night and rap on the shutter. She'll let me in. Then I'll be gone before morning."

"Let her know that Nick and I are safe. Tell her we'll be back soon."

She hugged Jammy, though she could tell that he felt uncomfortable. Jammy wasn't used to hugs from white people.

After shaking hands with Nick, Jammy took a few steps toward the door. Then he stopped. "Do you want some help getting into the loft?"

"We'll manage," said Charlotte. "You'd best be on your way."

She and Nick watched from the doorway as Jammy crossed the creek, using the trunk of the fallen cypress tree for a bridge. Just as he had first appeared emerging from a wall of green, he disappeared into it the same way.

# Chapter 22

THEY STOOD IN the flooded cabin, looking up at the loose
boards.

"I'll push those out of the way," said Nick, "then we can go
up."

Charlotte turned to him. "Someone may be up there now,
hiding in the loft."

"If there is, he's being mighty quiet."

"Wouldn't you be, if somebody was breaking into your
hiding place?"

"Are you serious? Do you really think someone may be up
there?"

"Yes."

"All right. Who is this fugitive lurking over our heads?"

"Elijah Cobman."

"Elijah Cobman! Your friend from the Mohawk Valley? You've told me a lot about him, but nothing to suggest he'd be hiding in a South Carolina swamp."

"Elijah deserted his regiment. He'll face a firing squad if he's caught."

"I see." Nick paused. "If he were in the loft, he'd hear you. He'd recognize your voice."

"But not yours. He might suspect a trap."

"Announce yourself, then. Tell him it's me with you."

"Of course. That's all I have to do." Raising her head, she called loud and clear, "Elijah! It's me, Charlotte! Nick's with me. It's safe."

Not a sound came from above.

She turned to Nick. "If he were here, he would answer."

"Let's go up and see what we find."

Nick raised his arms and shifted the loose boards aside. Lacing his fingers, he made a stirrup of his hands. "Up you go!"

As Charlotte set her foot in place and put her hands upon his shoulders, she felt a tremor come over him. The spark of energy he had shown seemed to have burned out.

Bracing her forearms on the frame, she pulled herself through and scrambled over the free boards onto the rough wooden floor. Spaces between the logs, where chinking had fallen out, admitted enough light for her to look around.

Overhead, the roof seemed tight; its overlapping wood shakes had kept out the rain. There was little headroom, only about four feet under the roof beam. But four feet was enough to allow them to sit up, at least in the middle of the loft.

A makeshift bed made of palmetto leaves took up half the floor space. The leaves were neatly placed, all pointing in the same direction, and stacked several layers high. On top lay a soldier's red coat.

"It's fine," she called to Nick. Crouching on the floorboards, she gave him a helping hand to haul himself up.

"Whew! I'm weak as a baby." He sat down heavily, panting to catch his breath.

After a moment, he saw the red coat. "So your friend has been here."

"Yes. That must be Elijah's coat."

"He's cut off the buttons."

For the first time, she noticed this. "So he did! I wonder why."

"Probably to conceal his identity. The name of his regiment is stamped on every button."

"It would be safer to sink the whole coat in the swamp."

"A coat makes a fair enough blanket if you've nothing better. This time of year, it's cold in the swamp at night."

"I suppose so." Charlotte set the free boards back in place. "We're safe here. Now you can rest."

Nick needed no urging. He flopped right onto the bed of

palmetto leaves. Charlotte pulled off his shoes. They were the fine leather shoes he had worn to the slave auction. Completely ruined.

Nick closed his eyes. Within seconds, his deep, regular breathing told Charlotte that he was asleep.

While he slept, she inspected the loft. From a wooden peg —actually a stick wedged between two logs—hung Elijah's white leather cross belts. On the floor lay a small Bible.

If Elijah had left for good, she was sure he would have taken his Bible with him. So he was either still using the loft, or he had been captured and would never return.

After inspecting the loft, she peered through a chink between the logs on the left side. All she saw were trees and vines. Then she looked through a chink on the right side, toward the creek. There was the fallen cypress tree that spanned its width. But now she saw something else, a big log that she hadn't noticed before. It was close to twenty feet long, half hidden in the rushes. The log was black, with deeply ridged bark. It must have been there all along, she thought, but hard to see except from above.

Charlotte lay down beside Nick and cuddled against him. He probably had a touch of ague. But if he slept for the rest of the day and all night, by tomorrow he'd be strong enough to manage the walk back to Charleston.

She yawned. Before leaving, she must write a note to warn Elijah that his secret cabin was not so secret as he thought. Since Jammy knew about it, others might as well. She could write her message in Elijah's Bible. But she didn't have a pencil. Wondering whether Nick had a pencil, she drifted to sleep.

A noise startled her awake. Not a loud noise, merely the sound of splashing right under where she lay. In the swamp's sleepy silence its effect was like the crack of a rifle. Someone had entered the cabin.

Fear seized her, followed quickly by relief. It must be Elijah.

She sat up and was about to call his name when some deep instinct stopped her.

For a moment there was no sound except the sloshing below and Nick's calm breathing next to her.

"Nobody's here." Billy's shrill voice cut through the silence. "I told you they'd head straight back to Charleston. We wasted precious time coming here."

"It was only a mile out of our way," Abner grumbled. "Worth a look, anyway. We can still overtake them on the wagon track. Our friend won't be too spry after three days in the cave."

"I reckon it's that young Quaker who freed him," said Billy.

Abner snorted. "Some Quaker! Damned Tory spy if you ask me. Well, you can give him back his hat when we catch them."

"That's not all I'm gonna give him. But Abner, there were

three people. Three sets of footprints. Our planter's son wore shoes. The Quaker wore boots. The third man was barefoot. Wonder who he was?"

"Maybe a runaway. Quakers and slaves get along pretty good."

"To tell the truth," said Billy, "I'm not sure that young man is a Quaker. I'm not even sure that he's a man."

"Now, what can you mean by that?"

"Remember that good-looking girl with our friend at the slave auction? She was just about that height. Same big brown eyes."

"Go on! You can't be serious!"

"Just an idea. Remember when we found the hat? I said there was something fishy."

"Come to think of it," said Abner, "that young Quaker had really pink cheeks for a boy."

Dear Lord, help us, Charlotte silently prayed. She looked at Nick lying on his back sound asleep, his mouth wide open. One good snore would finish them.

"Come on," said Billy. "Let's lose no more time."

Charlotte heard them leave the cabin. Cautiously she crawled over to a chink in the wall, and watched as they approached the fallen tree that bridged the creek. Where the water had receded there were patches of bare mud.

Neither man seemed aware of the big log that Charlotte had noticed from above, half hidden in the rushes. It was not until they reached the fallen tree bridging the creek that anything attracted their attention. Then both of them stopped. They bent over, obviously examining something in the mud.

A chill ran through her when she realized what they must be looking at: Jammy's footprints.

Abner scratched his head. Billy shrugged his shoulders. They both turned and looked back at the cabin.

They were too far away for her to hear their conversation, but she reckoned she knew what they were talking about. Three people had left the cave. One wore shoes, one wore boots, and the third was barefoot. The footprints of all three had led to the edge of a flooded region. In the water there would have been no tracks to follow.

Did Abner and Billy recognize the barefoot footprints? And if they did, were they wondering about the other two people who had left the cave?

Abner took a few steps toward the cabin. Billy followed, a pace or two behind. This time they would search thoroughly. If they found their way into the loft, there would be no escape.

Charlotte stayed where she was, frozen, hardly breathing. Nick moved and stretched in his sleep. "Shh!" she whispered.

Her eye was at the hole in the wall when the big log began to move. It moved on little crooked legs. Slowly.

Then suddenly it shot forward, straight for Billy.

It wasn't a log.

Her hand flew to her mouth as the creature lunged. Jaws

opened—jaws a yard long, with rows of jagged teeth. She heard the crunch of bone as the jaws snapped shut around Billy's thigh.

Billy screamed. Spray flew in all directions as the alligator dragged its prey into the swamp.

The taste of blood was in her mouth, and she realized that she had bitten down on her knuckle hard enough to break the skin.

"Billy!" Abner shouted. "Billy!"

Billy screamed one more time.

Abner fled. Arms flailing, he raced across the fallen tree and kept going.

Nick woke. He blinked. "Did I hear somebody yell?"

She opened her mouth but could not speak. Her fingers clutched his arm. She was quaking from head to toe.

"An alligator," she gasped, "got Billy!"

"My God!! What are you telling me?"

"They were here . . . Billy and Abner . . . they knew . . . about the cabin." She spoke in bursts, as if the words were being shaken out of her. "They left. Then they started back . . ."

He gripped both her hands. Gradually she told him the rest.

When she finished, he said, "We haven't seen the last of Abner."

"I don't think he'll ever come back. Abner ran as if all the devils of hell were after him."

"He'll be back. He's got too much to lose if he doesn't. He'll find his other friend. Then they'll return to look for me." Nick took her in his arms and held her while her racing heart slowed to normal.

"This cabin feels more like a death trap than a sanctuary," she said.

"It will soon be dark. We're safe until tomorrow. We have all night to remove this hardware." He pointed to his feet. Although Jammy had severed the ten-inch chain that joined his shackles, they were still on his ankles. "If I have to run, I'll be faster if I'm not wearing manacles and dragging links of chain."

She took the file from her satchel and handed it to him.

# Chapter 23

FOR A FEW MINUTES Nick wielded the file with vigor. But his energy soon ran out. Charlotte took over, and for the rest of the day they took turns, stopping only to share the last of the bread and cheese from her satchel. By sundown they had removed the shackle that encircled Nick's left ankle.

He took off his shoe and stocking and sat rubbing the skin, where the shackle had left red marks. After giving the leg a good stretch, he said, "I feel much better now. It's low tide and the creek is running clear. I'm going outside to fill the flask. Then I'll start on the other ankle."

He crawled over to the wall to peer outside. "I wonder where the alligator is?"

"We have nothing to fear from that particular alligator."

"I'd still like to know." Nick put his eye to the chink between the logs. "I don't see it." He hesitated. "But just a minute! Somebody's coming!"

Charlotte felt a burst of panic. "Not Abner!"

"No. It's an Indian."

"Let me see."

When Charlotte looked out, she saw a slim young man crossing the fallen tree that bridged the creek. He held a bow in his hand. On his shoulder he wore a quiver of arrows, and on his back a carrying basket. Nothing else about him looked Indian—not his brown hair pulled back in a pigtail, or his linsey-woolsey undershirt, or his army boots.

She let out a sigh of relief. "That's not an Indian. It's Elijah."

"Carrying a bow and arrows?"

"That doesn't surprise me."

For a few moments she lost sight of him. Then she heard a bump as something knocked against the floor of the loft. One of the loose boards rose, and the top of a ladder poked up.

"Elijah, it's me, Charlotte!" she shouted.

"What!"

She lifted the second loose board out of the way. An instant later, Elijah's head popped up over the edge of the floor. She couldn't help smiling at the astonishment on his face.

"Nick's here, too," she said.

The rest of Elijah ascended. He pulled up the ladder and

laid it under the eaves out of the way.

"Nick reached over and stuck out his hand. "Glad to meet you, Elijah. Charlotte's told me a lot about you."

Elijah shook Nick's hand. "And I've heard plenty about you."

So much for introductions, Charlotte thought. But nothing more was needed. It seemed so extraordinary that Nick and Elijah, two of the most important people in her life, had never met before. It was all because of the war. Sometimes war brought people together who otherwise never would have known each other, and sometimes it sent friends and loved ones far away.

"Elijah, where did you find the ladder?" Charlotte asked.

"When I discovered the cabin, it was inside, leaning against the wall. I suspected what it was for, so I tested the ceiling boards until I found the opening. When I'm away, I keep the ladder hidden in the undergrowth. When I'm here, I pull it up into the loft out of sight."

Elijah shrugged off his quiver and his carrying basket. "I'm used to shocks," he said, "but this beats anything." He shifted his gaze from Charlotte to Nick and then back to Charlotte. "How did you find me? The directions I gave weren't *that* good."

"I wasn't really looking for you. Finding the cabin was almost an accident." She shook her head. "It was Nick I was trying to find."

Elijah smiled. "Wherever I meet you . . . whenever I meet

you . . . you always seem to be searching for Nick."

"Well, this time I found him."

"I'd say he's lucky you did." Elijah looked again at Nick, his eyes registering the slave collar, the hand bolt, and the remaining shackle with its dangling links of chain. "What happened, Nick? You look like you've escaped from a dungeon."

"That's close enough. A couple of Over Mountain men had me chained in a cave. Charlotte rescued me."

"A lot has happened," Charlotte said, "since you left Charleston."

"I'd surely like to hear about it."

Elijah sat down on the loft floor, facing them, while Charlotte told him everything. She ended with the alligator making a meal of Billy.

When she had finished, he said, "And here I thought you were in Charleston, doing nothing more dangerous than lugging bundles of laundry while I sat here slapping mosquitoes and wondering how long I'd be stuck in the swamp."

"If you plan to stay in the swamp," Nick said, "you need to find a safer hiding place."

"I'm not staying," said Elijah. "I've had enough of hiding in the swamp. Living here could drive a person mad. It's everything all together: the mosquitoes, the snakes, the alligators, the rising mist, and the smell. There's plenty of game, but I can't cook what I kill. If I lit a fire, somebody would see the smoke. The first night I was here, I snared a muskrat."

He grimaced. "Did you ever eat raw muskrat?"

"No," Charlotte and Nick both replied.

"You don't want to. After that experience, I lived on oysters and hardtack. The day I finished the hardtack was when I decided to leave." He opened his basket. "But look at this! I have food for three days on the trail, as well as a good bow and twenty arrows with metal tips."

"Where did you get all that?" asked Charlotte.

"From Creeks who live on the Edisto River. I traded the pewter buttons from my uniform for the food and the weapons."

"Clever," said Nick. "I saw you'd cut off the buttons, but never thought of that."

"Try this." Elijah handed Charlotte and Nick each a strip of dried meat from the basket.

Charlotte sank her teeth into it. "Mm!"

"Very good," said Nick.

"Smoked turkey."

When Charlotte had finished chewing her mouthful, she said, "Elijah, I don't blame you for wanting to leave the swamp. But where can you go?"

"I'm going west to live with the Cherokees. In the mountains, the air is fresh and clean. There's a village called Chickamauga where I'll be welcome."

"Wasn't the deserter you told me about captured on his way to Cherokee territory?" Charlotte asked.

"Sergeant Malcolm. Yes. He was caught because he didn't

know the trails and mountain passes. But I do. I travelled through that country on my way to Carleton Island."

Nick said, "The British offer big rewards to the Indians for turning in deserters."

"I know that, but the Cherokees won't turn me in. Last fall, I helped save the life of a Cherokee warrior. They won't forget that." Elijah began to drag the ladder from under the eaves. "I might as well start out now."

"No need to rush," Nick protested. "There's room for three to sleep here tonight."

"I didn't plan to stay for the night. I just came back to pick up my Bible. It was a gift from my mother, so I don't want to leave it behind. If I hurry, there's a pine ridge I can reach to make camp before dark."

The Bible lay on the floor close by. Charlotte handed it to him.

After putting the Bible into his basket, Elijah gathered up his gear, put the ladder in place, and scrambled down. When he reached the bottom, he waved his farewell. "If you're ever in Chickamauga, come to see me."

Charlotte and Nick watched him leave, not crossing the creek but heading north, the opposite direction.

"I know that Elijah will be better off living in a Cherokee village than hiding in the swamp," said Charlotte. "But what use will Cherokees have for a man who refuses to fight? He's told me how he feels."

"He can be useful in other ways. Hunting. Negotiating."

Nick swung himself onto the ladder. "I'll fill the flask before the tide turns. If I delay, the water will be too brackish to drink."

When Nick returned, he said, "There's a big alligator lying on the creek bank. It looks like it ate recently."

"Then it won't be hungry for weeks." Her tone was so matter-of-fact that she shocked herself. Crawling to a chink in the wall, she looked down. There it was. Black. Armour-plated. Engorged.

"Do you suppose it digests everything? Shoes? Clothes? The hat Mrs. Doughty loaned me was in Billy's pack." She took her eye from the hole and turned to Nick. "I was just thinking about something. Before I left her house, Mrs. Doughty said she didn't know why God created alligators. Well, I don't know either. But I can tell you I'm mighty glad he did."

At dawn they were ready to leave. Nick had rid his ankles of the shackles. But he still had the hand bolt fastened to his left wrist and the slave collar around his neck.

"If we head south," he said, "sooner or later we'll come to the wagon track."

"But, Nick, that's exactly where Abner expects us to go."

"Then we must find another way. If we take our bearings from the sun, sooner or later, we'll get back to Charleston."

"Can we do it in one day?"

"That depends on how many bogs and ponds we have to

skirt around. Tonight we may have to sleep in the swamp."

She shuddered. "I don't want to spend the night outdoors in the swamp. Anything but that."

"Then let's get started."

Nick moved aside the loose boards and put the ladder in place. Before following him down, Charlotte took one last look around the loft. Elijah's buttonless red coat lay on the palmetto leaves, and Nick's severed shackles on the floor.

When both of them had descended, Charlotte asked, "What shall we do with the ladder?"

"Let's leave it in place, with the ceiling boards pushed out of the way, in case someone else comes along who needs a dry place to stay."

"Yes," she agreed. "Let's do that. When the next person comes here, I wonder what he'll make of what he sees. Will he guess at the stories the red coat and the shackles have to tell?"

They waded from the cabin into dappled sunlight. On the creek bank the alligator lay basking.

"It's not hungry. It's not hungry," Charlotte told herself. Certainly it didn't look hungry. As they walked by, its leathery eyelids flicked over its bulbous eyes. No other part of the gator moved. On its sculpted face it wore a yard-long crooked smile.

# Chapter 24

THE GROUND WAS spongy but firm as long as they were under the trees. Nick, in the lead, seemed confident that they were walking in the right direction. Charlotte was not so sure. One cypress tree looked much like another. But she suppressed her suspicion that they were lost and followed doggedly after.

She didn't know how long they had been walking—maybe an hour—when they came to a field of mud that looked half a mile wide.

"Do we go through it or around it?" she asked.

"Let's try going through it. Going around it would take an hour."

They had walked only a few yards, their feet squelching, when Nick stopped and turned toward her. "I think I've lost my shoes."

There he stood in mud up to his ankles.

"We'd better find them," she said, "if only to save the buckles."

They groped in the muck and pulled out the shoes. Under an inch-thick coat of mud, they barely resembled shoes any longer. Nick carried them until he and Charlotte reached higher ground. Then he borrowed her knife to scrape them before putting them back on his feet.

Charlotte felt thankful for her stout boots, with their waterproof coating of beeswax, tallow and tar. Through everything, her feet were dry.

On their left rose a wooded hill.

"If we climb to the top," Charlotte suggested, "we might get a better idea of problems that lie ahead."

"That might help," Nick agreed.

As they climbed, the wooded slope began to look familiar. This might, she thought, be the same hill that she had mistaken for an island when she stood on the porch of Hewitt's Inn.

Reaching the top, she saw Hewitt's Inn below them, half a mile to the south. So all their slogging through the swamp had taken them in a circle. At this rate, they'd never reach Charleston in just one day.

From the top of the hill, Charlotte and Nick also had a

perfect view of the wagon track, which was mostly above water once again.

Approaching from the northwest was a wagon drawn by a pair of mules. Two men sat on the seat at the front. A black tarpaulin, sagging in the middle, covered the wagon bed.

"That wagon's empty," said Nick. "It's probably on its way back to Charleston after delivering its load—supplies for General Greene, most likely."

"Maybe it will stop at the inn."

"It probably will, but just long enough for the men to have a meal and rest the mules. They'll want to get the wagon back to town tonight."

A brilliant idea sprang into Charlotte's mind. "Let's hitch a ride."

Nick snorted. "You can't be serious! With a slave collar around my neck and a hand bolt locked to one wrist, I need to stay out of sight. But even if there were no danger in being seen, who would offer either of us a ride, the way we look? We're filthy."

"I didn't mean we'd *ask* for a ride. If the men go into the inn, we can crawl under the tarpaulin and relax all the way back to Charleston. No more mosquitoes. No more bogs. And we'll be back in Charleston tonight."

"You clever girl!" His eyes brightened. "We can jump off when we reach the outskirts of Charleston. It will be dark by then. No one will see us." He squeezed her hand. "Let's go!"

Descending the wooded hill, they briefly lost sight of the

wagon. But when they reached the bottom and watched from the cover of the trees, there it was, coming to a stop in front of the inn, only about fifty feet from where they stood.

The carters climbed down from their seat. They hitched the wagon to a post and went inside, leaving the mules, still in harness, munching the greenery that grew beside the track.

Nick and Charlotte approached the wagon, careful to keep it between themselves and the inn, in case somebody happened to look out the window.

"I'll release the tailgate," said Nick, "then I'll climb under the tarpaulin and lift up an edge for you to crawl under."

She nodded. "Hurry!"

He crept to the back of the wagon, undid a couple of catches—one on each side—and carefully let down the tailgate. Then he climbed onto the wagon bed and disappeared under the tarpaulin. A moment later, one edge rose. She saw his arm holding it up in an inverted V, like the entrance to a little tent.

Charlotte dashed across the open ground that lay between the trees and the wagon. Nick grabbed her hand to pull her up. Then she dived under the tarpaulin while Nick lifted the tailgate and fastened it in place. When he dropped the tarpaulin, it lay on them like a collapsed tent.

"What's that bad smell?" Charlotte asked. "Like rotten eggs."

"Gunpowder."

"It doesn't smell like gunpowder."

"Unfired gunpowder doesn't smell the same as burnt powder. What you're smelling is saltpetre and sulphur." They lay side by side. "Now," said Nick, "you crawl over to one side, and I'll go to the other. We don't want to make a lump in the middle."

It was black as night under the tarpaulin. As soon as Charlotte reached her side of the wagon bed, she lifted the edge of the tarpaulin just an inch to admit a little light and air. As she squirmed about, trying to find a comfortable position on the wagon bed, her hand brushed a smooth sheet of paper.

Curious, she picked it up, and then she lifted the edge of the tarpaulin another inch so that she could read the writing. The paper appeared to be an invoice or bill of some kind—not the sort of thing she would expect to find lying on the floorboards of a wagon. The writing was in a neat clerical hand:

### Bill of Lading

Rifles, 6 crates. 10 rifles per crate
Gunpowder, four barrels
For Delivery to General Nathanael Greene
Benbow's Ferry

She turned over the paper. On the other side was a scribbled note in pencil:

Load shipment 19 February. End of 2nd Watch.

Warehouse foot of Broad Street.

Speak to Lewis Morley and no one else.

This took a moment to sink in.

It was hard to believe. But the words admitted no other interpretation. Lewis Morley, a staunch Loyalist, was involved in shipping arms to the rebels.

She slipped the paper between the pages of the Bible that Mrs. Doughty had given her. As she put it into her pouch, she heard men's voices approaching. Charlotte dropped the edge of the tarpaulin and lay still.

She heard the men untie the mules. The wagon gave a slight lurch as the carters climbed onto their seat.

"Giddy-up!" one called out.

The wagon jolted forward. At first she felt as if her bones would shake loose with the bouncing and jouncing. But she got used to it. Lying there with nothing else to do, she had plenty of time to think.

There were two possibilities. First, Mr. Morley might always have been a secret rebel, a man who truly believed in the goals of the revolution. Second, he might be doing this just for the money. Importing goods from abroad had made him rich. Selling rifles and gunpowder to the rebels would make him richer still.

Charlotte really didn't care about his motives. His actions were what counted. And as she mulled over the consequences of his actions, she thought of Jammy.

Morley's treason, when it came to light, would turn Jammy's situation upside down. If he applied to Southern Command as an escaped slave owned by a rebel, he would not be sent back to his owner. Instead, he would be offered a chance to work on fortifications or to join a regiment like the Black Pioneers or the Black Dragoons. And at the end of one year he would be awarded a General Birch certificate guaranteeing his future as a free man.

She must get this news to Jammy before he left Charleston. She could hardly wait to tell him that now there was no reason for him to flee. He and Phoebe need not part.

Hurry! Hurry! She silently urged the plodding mules. But her urging had no effect.

She couldn't relax, not holding such a secret. She burned to tell Nick.

Many long hours went slowly by. It was dark under the tarpaulin. Even when she raised its edge to admit a slit of light, the wagon's solid wooden side kept her from seeing where she was. She had no idea how far they had travelled until the light outside began to fade and the approach of night told her that Charleston must be near.

It was completely dark when she felt a tap on the shoulder. Nick had crawled over to her side of the wagon.

"Now!"

The tarpaulin shifted. A click, followed by another click, told her that Nick had released the tailgate. The wagon gave a bounce when he jumped.

Then she jumped too, half rolling from the open end. Nick pulled her to her feet and off the track.

The wagon did not stop. To the men seated at the front, their passengers' departure must have felt like a couple of bumps on the rutted track. When the men arrived at the stable, they might wonder how they could have forgotten to fasten the tailgate. Apart from that, Nick and Charlotte's presence would leave no mark.

Charlotte looked up. The sky was full of stars.

"Where are we?" she asked.

"At the Charleston boundary. We're inside the hornwork wall that crosses from the Ashley River to the Cooper."

A breeze was blowing from the harbour, fresh against her skin. Over the sound of small creatures scuttling in the grass, she heard the rippling chime of distant bells—the bells of St. Michael's Church, each singing with a different voice.

"Eleven o'clock." Nick put his arms around her and held her for a minute without speaking. Then he kissed her. "We've done it!" he said, and kissed her again. "Now let's get back to Mrs. Doughty's house."

"Just a minute. I have something to show you. A paper I found on the wagon floor." She pulled the bill of lading from her satchel and held it under his nose.

"I can't read it. It's too dark."

"It's a bill of lading that lists six crates of rifles, ten rifles to a crate, and four barrels of gunpowder to be delivered to General Nathanael Greene at Benbow's Ferry." She stopped for breath. "And on the back there's a note in pencil that says, 'Load shipment 19 February. End of 2nd Watch. Warehouse foot of Broad Street. Speak to Lewis Morley and no one else.'"

"Good God!" said Nick. "Put that paper right back in your satchel. I have to show this to Southern Command. You know what it means, don't you?"

"It means freedom for Jammy."

"Yes, it does. We certainly owe it to Jammy to make sure of that. But much more than one boy's freedom is involved."

# Chapter 25

THEY WALKED HAND-IN-HAND to Stoll's Alley through the quiet streets. At the front door, Charlotte took her house key from her satchel. They tiptoed inside, not wanting to waken the household.

Nick struck a spark with his flint and steel to make a fire in the front room fireplace. Charlotte lit a candle. By its light Nick read the bill of lading. He read both front and back.

"It seems that Lewis Morley isn't the upstanding citizen everyone thought him."

"I never thought he was upstanding. Look how treated Phoebe. How upstanding was that?"

"It's his public reputation, not his private morals that I'm talking about. Everyone thinks he's a loyal subject of King George." Nick tapped the bill of lading with his finger. "Don't say a word about this to anyone."

"Not to Phoebe? Not to Jammy?"

"Not to anyone. In the morning I'll show this paper to Southern Command."

"When you've done that, may I tell Phoebe and Jammy."

"No, my dear. There must be absolute secrecy. If word leaks out, the people involved may simply disappear. They'll escape before they can be caught. Morley's an important man. He may not be the only important man to have a hand in this. We know supply wagons reach General Greene's army and Francis Marion's swamp dodgers in the interior. Some wagons go all the way to George Washington's forces in Virginia."

"Why doesn't the army intercept them?"

"Southern Command's troops are spread too thin. Besides that, there are hundreds of rebel sympathizers ready to turn a blind eye, even when they have an idea what's happening. Wagons load in the middle of the night. We don't know who the suppliers or the organizers are." His finger tapped the paper again. "This is the only breakthrough there's been.

"First thing tomorrow, as soon as I've bathed and changed my clothes, I'll visit a locksmith to remove the rest of the hardware. I mustn't attract attention when I take in this paper. Even at Southern Command there may be traitors. There's more than one Benedict Arnold in this world."

"I know about Benedict Arnold. Everybody despises him, even though he's on our side."

"Arnold's not on anybody's side but his own. He's been a schemer all his life. He schemed to win George Washington's support to make him Commander of West Point. As soon as he took command, he started negotiations to hand it over to the British for twenty thousand pounds."

"That's a fortune!"

"If the plot had succeeded, he'd be a very wealthy man, and Britain would be winning the war."

"You sound sure of that."

"I am sure. Here's why. In the North, the British commander General Clinton has an army of thousands of soldiers. In the South, General Cornwallis has thousands more. But they can't function as an effective fighting force as long as George Washington's troops hold the territory in between. West Point is a strategic location on the Hudson River. If England held West Point, Clinton and Cornwallis would be able to unite their forces in a single campaign."

"Is Morley as dangerous as Benedict Arnold?"

"There's no telling how dangerous he is. I'm sure he's not acting alone. What if there's a conspiracy to hand over Charleston to the rebels?" Nick looked at the bill of lading again. "This is the most important document I've ever held in my hands, even during the years I was a courier. Sweetheart, I'll tell Southern Command that you found it. This makes you some kind of hero."

"I didn't do anything except pick up a piece of paper," she said modestly, though secretly thrilled at the idea of being recognized as a heroine.

Nick stretched. "I can do nothing until morning. We might as well get some sleep."

"I'm too excited to sleep," Charlotte said as she dragged their mattresses onto the front room rug. "Can't I just give a hint that Jammy won't be a hunted man much longer?"

"Not even the smallest hint." Nick stretched out on his mattress. "Don't breathe a word of this to anyone."

At daybreak Noah woke them, crying to be fed.

Charlotte and Nick waited to give Phoebe enough time to take care of him, and then a little longer until they heard Mrs. Doughty's footsteps on the stairs.

When Charlotte opened the door to the kitchen, there was Mrs. Doughty pouring flour into a big, yellow mixing bowl. Over by the window, Phoebe sat with Noah at her breast. Phoebe and Mrs. Doughty looked up. Their eyes opened wide.

Phoebe gave a shriek. "You're back. You found Nick!"

"God be thanked!" There was a tremble in Mrs. Doughty's voice and a smile on her face. "Nick looks like a man of mud, and thee's no better."

"I dredged him from the very depths of the swamp," said Charlotte. "Unluckily, it cost me your husband's hat."

"Do not trouble thee about a hat. I thank the Lord for thy safe return. We'll eat breakfast, and then set up the bathtub."

"No breakfast for me," said Nick. "But I need a bath. It's important that I report to Headquarters as soon as I can."

"There's water in the rain barrel for two baths," said Mrs. Doughty.

While Nick was fetching the water, Charlotte set up the tin hipbath and the wicker privacy screen in the kitchen. As soon as he returned, he disappeared behind the screen with a full bucket of water, not taking time to warm it over the fire.

While Nick was taking a bath on one side of the screen and Mrs. Doughty was cooking grits on the other, Patience, Charity and Joseph came down the stairs. Now there were eight people, including the baby, in the small kitchen. They made so much confusion that there might as well have been eighteen. Charlotte shepherded the little Doughtys into the front room.

In a few minutes Phoebe joined them, leaving Noah in his cradle. As soon as she had shut the door, she asked, "Did you see Jammy?"

"I was about to ask you the same thing. Has he been here?"

"No." She stared hard at Charlotte. "You have seen him, haven't you?"

"Yes. In the swamp."

Before Charlotte or Phoebe had a chance to say more, Nick emerged from the kitchen clean-shaven, his freshly washed hair tied at the back with a black ribbon bow. He wore a blue coat and grey breeches with gleaming brass knee buckles. He would have looked very smart if there hadn't been a slave collar around his neck and a hand bolt clamping one wrist.

"Apart from the hardware," said Charlotte, "you look like a new man."

When he took a step toward her, she took a step back, holding out her hands palm forward to fend him off. "Don't touch me! I'm too dirty!"

He kissed her anyway. "I'm off to the locksmith, and then straight to Headquarters."

"The locksmith may mistake you for an escaped convict."

"He won't. He knows me too well, and he knows I work for Southern Command. It's part of a locksmith's profession to be discreet. He won't even ask about the collar and hand bolt."

Nick crossed the room to the front door. With his hand on the latch, he said, "I'll be back as soon as I can, but there's no telling how long this will take."

He left her then, shutting the door behind him.

Gone again. It was absurd to fear for his safety every moment he was out of her sight. But she remembered what happened the last time they parted. He had said he would see her "in an hour or two." And look what happened!

"Miss Charlotte . . ." Phoebe's voice broke in upon her thoughts. "If Jammy was coming here, I can think of only one thing that would stop him." She took a deep breath. "Slave catchers."

Charlotte looked away. She could think of one other unattractive possibility. However, Jammy was far more likely to be captured by slave catchers than eaten by an alligator.

Phoebe's voice trembled. "Mrs. Doughty told me there was a reward."

"Yes. It was advertised in the *Royal Gazette*. Twenty pounds. Payable if Jammy was delivered to the workhouse."

"Do you think Jammy may be imprisoned in the workhouse?"

"Yes."

Charlotte's thoughts raced.

Jammy had started out for Charleston three days ago. If slave catchers caught him, it would have been yesterday, maybe the day before. How much time normally passed between capture and execution? How long would it take for Southern Command to act upon Nick's information? Jammy might be dead before the truth about Lewis Morley's activities came to light. Much good a General Birch certificate would do him then!

From the kitchen came Mrs. Doughty's voice: "Breakfast is ready."

"Phoebe," Charlotte said calmly, "the first thing to do is to find Jammy. If he's being held at the workhouse, we must find a way to get him released."

"There is no way." Phoebe began to weep. "You know that. He's run away three times."

Charlotte grabbed Phoebe's hands. She wanted to say, *But there is a way!* Already she realized that this would be the hardest secret she'd ever had to keep.

# Chapter 26

"I'VE NEVER BEEN inside the workhouse," Phoebe said, "but Jammy has. He told me about it. Mr. Morley paid the warden a shilling for his correction. They took him into the whipping room, where the walls are two-feet thick and filled with sand to muffle the screaming." Phoebe's lower lip trembled. "There was a crane, with a pulley. The warden chained Jammy's feet to bolts in the floor. Men hoisted the crane until his body was so stretched out he thought he'd be pulled apart. And then they beat him."

"I've never been there either," said Charlotte, "and it's not a place I want to go. But if Jammy is imprisoned there, the sooner we know, the better."

Phoebe wiped her eyes with the back of her hand. "If they've taken Jammy there, I don't know any way you can free him. The only person who could do that is Mr. Morley."

"Let's cross that bridge when we come to it," Charlotte said, wishing she could at least hint that Mr. Morley would soon lose his rights over Jammy. "The first thing is to find out if Jammy's there. And if he isn't there, where is he?"

Not voicing her fear that Jammy might already be dead, Charlotte settled her good blue cloak about her shoulders. "I don't know when I'll be back. There's laundry to deliver, so if you could—"

"But I can't. I still don't have a certificate that says I'm free. I won't be able to get one until I have that deed of manumission from the lawyer. If I go out on the street, the slave patrol might pick me up if I'm not with a white person. Then you might be looking for me at the workhouse, too."

"Oh," Charlotte muttered, "I should have remembered." What a world we live in! she thought. It's not only unjust, it's ridiculous.

It was a long walk from Stoll's Alley to the workhouse, which was located in the northwest part of Charleston. As she turned from Church Street onto Queen Street, Charlotte could see it from blocks away, its great bulk looming above the surrounding buildings. With its massive towers and barred windows, the workhouse matched her idea of an ogre's castle—a place of torment, darkness, and danger.

Behind the building, a brick wall enclosed the workhouse yard, where the gallows were erected. The gallows stood taller than the wall.

The building's proper name was the House of Correction. Charlotte did not know why everyone called it the workhouse. No one imprisoned there ever did any work. They were sent to the workhouse for punishment, which was politely called "correction." It was just for black people. Every level of offense committed by a black person—from running away to murder—was dealt with there.

She knew that white offenders had a courthouse of their own as well as prisons of their own. And the rules were different.

The street was filled with people. The closer she came to the workhouse, the more the crowd grew. Charlotte was jostled and bumped. Through the slit in the skirt of her gown she kept a tight hold on her pocket.

When they reached the building, she let herself be carried along by the crowd. There was a crush of people pushing and shoving in their hurry to enter. No doubt something important was about to happen in that stern, forbidding place. Everything seemed ominous. She thought of Jammy and felt afraid.

The crowd forged ahead through a pair of open doors into an entrance hall, and then up a wide staircase into another hall, where a set of double doors stood open. Everyone was jostling and shoving to get into the room beyond those doors.

At the entrance, Charlotte hesitated. By her sudden stop she caused the man behind her to bump her shoulder rather hard.

"Beg your pardon, Miss," he said.

The man's companion was speaking to him. Charlotte's ears caught one sentence: "I'm interested in hearing what Lewis Morley will say."

Lewis Morley! What would he say about *what*? It must have something to do with Jammy. The man whom Charlotte had overheard obviously expected Mr. Morley to be present. But would he be? Nick had taken the bill of lading to Southern Command two hours ago. A lot could happen in two hours. Mr. Morley might be a prisoner in the Provost Dungeon by now.

The room Charlotte was entering had a dais at the back wall, with a long table standing on the dais. There were two water pitchers on the table, and four tumblers evenly spaced along its length. A man in livery stood at one end of the table. There was a closed door behind it in the back wall. In front of the dais was a boxed-off area just big enough to hold one person.

A dozen rows of benches took up most of the room. The benches were packed with people. Most were men, and all were white. The room smelled of sweat.

She took a seat in the back row, hoping not to be noticed.

After a few minutes, the man in livery announced, "All upstanding!" At these words, everybody stood up.

Four white men now entered in single file, marched up the aisle between the rows of benches to the table on the dais, and took their seats facing the benches. Then everyone sat down again. It felt a bit like church.

Three of the men at the table wore well-cut frockcoats and ruffled shirts. The fourth man was differently garbed. He wore a black robe with little crossed tabs for a tie, and a long, curly white wig. In his hand he held a silver-headed gavel, with which he now rapped on the table.

"The Magistrates and Freeholders Court is in session," he announced. "This morning, four slaves will be sentenced. Correction will immediately follow."

That man's the magistrate, Charlotte decided. The other three are the freeholders—men of property.

"Produce the first slave," the magistrate commanded.

The door behind the dais opened. Through the doorway two guards entered with their prisoner between them, in chains. It was Jammy.

Charlotte's heart began to thump with excitement. Jammy was alive! But could she save him?

He was still barefoot and half naked, his exposed skin still covered with mosquito bites and dried mud. Dozens of fresh welts stood out in reddish purple lines, vivid against the mud. His right eye was swollen shut, and his cheek was puffy.

"Will the petitioner come forward?" the magistrate said.

Nothing happened.

"Is Lewis Morley present in the court?"

The people seated on the benches stirred and looked about.

"Is Lewis Morley present in the court?" the magistrate repeated. Still no one stepped forward.

The magistrate banged the table with his gavel and asked for the third time.

"Is Lewis Morley present in the court?" He waited. He banged the table again. "We cannot proceed in the absence of the petitioner."

The other men at the table nodded solemnly. A buzz of whispers rose from the benches.

A reprieve! It seemed that Jammy was safe as long as Mr. Morley did not appear. Although he would return to the horrors of the workhouse, he would escape hanging for the time being. And time was on his side.

"Mr. Morley received due notice of this proceeding," said the magistrate. "Does anyone in the courtroom possess information to explain his absence?"

Charlotte stirred in her seat. Did Morley's absence mean that he was already under arrest? It might mean that. It might not. Other reasons were possible. An accident. Sudden illness. An emergency at Morley's warehouse.

Suddenly a gentleman two rows in front of Charlotte stood up. He wore a grey frockcoat and a white periwig with a little pigtail at the nape. "Your worship," he said. "I represent Mr. Morley."

The magistrate banged his gavel. "Then can you enlighten this court as to why he is not here?"

"No, Your Worship, I cannot. But I have a signed and notarized deposition prepared by Mr. Morley for presentation in the event that the demands of business should prevent him from attending."

"Produce the deposition," said the magistrate.

The man in livery took from the gentleman a folded, sealed document. He handed it to the magistrate.

The magistrate broke the seal, unfolded the document, and read it silently. He raised his eyes. "This appears to be in order. The court may proceed with sentencing."

Charlotte sat stunned. For a breathless moment she had thought that Jammy was safe, if only for today. Now that moment had passed. A vision came to her of Jammy mounting the scaffold, a crowd gathered to watch him die.

She rose to her feet. Everyone's eyes were upon her as she stuck out her chin and mustered a firm voice.

"Your Worship, the sentencing must not proceed."

# Chapter 27

THE MAGISTRATE RAISED his head and looked in her direction. She was not afraid. She felt strong and full of purpose.

"If you wish to know why the sentencing must not proceed, then send a messenger to the Headquarters of Southern Command. For the present, that is all I am free to say."

She took a deep breath. Oh, what a chance she had taken! What if something had happened to Nick on his way to Headquarters? What if the bill of lading had not been evidence enough? What if she was speaking too soon? It was possible that Lewis Morley had not yet been arrested.

From the way people looked at her, she supposed that everyone in the courtroom thought she was insane. Voices rose all around.

The magistrate banged the table with his gavel. "Order!"

He addressed Charlotte. "You could be charged for disrupting the order of this court."

"Yes, Your Worship. I understand. Charge me if you must. But at least, delay sentencing for the time being."

"What is your name, young woman?"

"Charlotte Schyler."

"Where do you live?"

"Stoll's Alley."

She heard laughter. "Stoll's Alley! Ha, ha, ha!"

The magistrate frowned. For a moment he and Charlotte looked into each other's eyes. He cleared his throat.

"The court will send a messenger to Southern Command. In the meantime, we shall proceed with the other cases. Young woman, you are not to leave this courtroom without my permission." Raising his hand, he pointed to Jammy. "Remove the prisoner."

Jammy was standing with his mouth hanging open, staring at Charlotte. The look on his face was one of total amazement. He remained staring at her over his shoulder as the guards led him away.

Charlotte sat down. She had done what needed to be done. And she had done it without revealing the evidence of the bill of lading. How long would it take for a message to come back from Headquarters? And what would that message be?

Her hands, she noticed, were trembling. She grabbed the edges of her cloak and willed the trembling to stop.

The next prisoner was a male slave—field hand, age twenty-five—accused of murdering another slave in a quarrel over a woman. After hearing the evidence, the panel of freeholders found him guilty, and the magistrate sentenced him to hang.

Then came the trial of a female house servant—cook, age fifty-one—found guilty of attempting to poison her master and his family. She, too, received a death sentence.

The last trial was of a runaway—male, age twenty—who, like Jammy, had made two previous escape attempts. For him as well, the sentence was death, the ultimate correction.

The session ended. The magistrate dismissed the court. Since the sentences were to be carried out immediately, there was a swift exodus of spectators as they rushed outside to secure a good viewing spot from which to watch the hangings.

The three freeholders were also in a hurry to go. In the almost empty courtroom, Charlotte heard them explain to the magistrate that they depended on the incoming tide to help bear their schooners upriver to their plantations.

Ignoring Charlotte, the magistrate now busied himself with a pile of papers in front of him on the table.

Charlotte waited, alone on the back bench. After a few minutes, she heard a loud cheer from outside. That must be the first prisoner being hanged. The warden certainly hadn't wasted any time getting on with the executions. "God have mercy," she prayed, hoping that the poor man would have better luck in the next life than he'd had in this.

Footsteps pounded up the stairs. Turning her head, she saw a man in livery enter the courtroom. He went straight to the magistrate and handed him a folded paper closed with a red wax seal.

The magistrate snapped the seal, unfolded the paper, and read. He shook his head and sighed when he had finished. Then he raised his head and looked directly at Charlotte.

"You may approach the bench."

Since there were twelve rows of benches, she had no idea which one he meant.

He must have sensed her confusion, for his stern countenance softened. "Come forward, young woman. Wherever I am sitting is the bench."

This did not make a great deal of sense to Charlotte, but the failure of things to make sense was becoming too common for her to question any longer. She walked up to the table, and when he directed her to take a seat, she sat down on the front bench, facing him.

"It appears that Mr. Morley is under arrest. He has been taken to the basement of the Exchange, the Provost Dungeon. Charges of assisting the enemy have been laid against him. I cannot imagine how someone like you could have anticipated this. Do you want to tell me?"

"No. I cannot." Charlotte kept her countenance smooth,

not showing her relief. "But it seems to me that you must let Jammy go free."

A frown knitted the magistrate's brow. "In South Carolina a man is presumed innocent until proven guilty. The sentencing of this slave cannot take place during the present circumstances. It must wait for the result of Mr. Morley's trial. Yet this hardly means I must order the prisoner's release."

"Why does he need to remain here? Let me take him. I lodge at the home of Mrs. Doughty, a Quaker woman of sound reputation. Send to her. I'm sure she will vouch for me. My husband, Nicholas Schyler, is employed at the Civilian Department of Southern Command. He will give his bond if you release Jammy into our custody."

The magistrate looked down at the paper and said under his breath, "Lewis Morley, of all people!" Then he leaned back in his chair, looking suddenly weary.

"You know this slave, Jammy, I presume?"

"I do. He is a young man of good character. He won't run away. Why should he? In a few days, or maybe weeks, he'll be eligible to apply for the General Birch certificate. But in the meantime, it's cruel and unnecessary to keep him locked up in this horrible place."

"The purpose of the Magistrates and Freeholders Court is to keep blacks under submission and to protect slave owners' property rights. It is not a court of justice or a court of mercy. Rarely is there opportunity for the exercise of either."

Charlotte heard him mutter something about the gentle

rain from heaven upon the earth beneath. Then he stood up.

"Wait here. I'll summon a clerk and send a messenger to Mrs. Doughty. If she agrees to take responsibility for the slave Jammy, that will suffice."

# Chapter 28

BAREFOOT, BATTERED, and muddy, Jammy was wearing the same torn breeches that he had worn when hiding in the swamp. He walked between Mrs. Doughty, in her black Quaker habit and coal-scuttle hat, and Charlotte, in her blue cloak. They made an odd-looking trio. It didn't surprise Charlotte that they received many a sideways glance on their walk to Stoll's Alley.

Before Jammy was well inside the front door, Phoebe, looking as fresh as a flower in her neat homespun dress and white apron, ran to him with a shriek and embraced him, dirt and all. The children stared.

"I said I was comin' back," said Jammy. Phoebe, sobbing against him, did not answer.

At once, Charlotte spotted Nick standing by the kitchen door, grinning and shaking his head at the same time. She ran to him. He put an arm around her and pulled her close to his side.

"Sweetheart, you've had a busy day. I was at Headquarters when the Magistrate's message arrived. The messenger told us that a young woman had stood up in court and *commanded* the magistrate not to proceed with sentencing. That was the word he used. 'Commanded.' I knew the young woman must be you. I wish I'd been there to see it. But, darling, you were taking a chance."

"I had my fingers crossed." Charlotte smiled. "If Morley hadn't been arrested, I would have looked an utter fool ... if not actually insane. But I was lucky."

Jammy, his arms still around Phoebe and his chin resting on the top of her head, was smiling too. "I'm the lucky one, 'cause I'm still alive, and Charlotte says that in one year I'm gonna be free."

"This is a wonderful day," said Charlotte. "But I'm glad it's over." She turned to Nick. "What was the reaction at Southern Command when you showed them the bill of lading?"

"Complete shock. But the evidence left no room for doubt. The commanding officer sent a platoon to arrest Morley. Naturally, I went along to observe. We went first to his warehouse at the foot of Broad Street. The foreman said Mr. Morley wouldn't be in until later because he had to go to the Magistrates and Freeholders Court to give his deposition about a runaway slave. The moment I heard this, I felt sure the slave was Jammy.

"It was just eight o'clock, too early for court to be in session. The captain of the squad thought Morley would still be at home, so he led us directly to his house.

"The butler answered the door. When he saw the soldiers with their muskets and the captain with his sword, he went lickety-split to fetch Morley. In a couple of minutes Morley appeared, already dressed for his morning in court. It seems he fully intended to be there; he'd prepared the deposition just as a precaution, which was a common practice with him.

"When the captain told him he was under arrest for assisting the enemy, he looked too shocked to speak. But he did speak, and I've never before heard such defiance. 'Sir,' he said, 'you have received false information. I am, and always have been, a true and faithful subject of His Majesty the King.'

"Then the captain read the charge and said that he had orders to take Morley to the Provost Dungeon. Morley looked furious, but he had dignity. 'Sir,' he said, 'there is no need for your men to lay their hands on me.' And off they went.

"Mrs. Morley had come downstairs by this time. As the soldiers marched her husband away, she started moaning that she didn't know what would become of her and her children."

Phoebe, now released from Jammy's arms, was wiping tears from her cheeks when a whimper from the direction of Noah's cradle sent her hurrying into the kitchen.

"I think all of us are hungry," said Mrs. Doughty. "So I'm going to cook up a mess of grits. And then I'll look for some clothes that will fit Jammy." She turned to him. "Unless thee objects to dressing like a Friend?"

"That'll be just fine, ma'am. But first I want to clean up."

"Thee needs a bath," she agreed. "Nowadays, it seems that everybody who comes to my house reeks of the swamp."

Jammy cleaned up very nicely, Charlotte thought. Phoebe, so clever with her needle, turned one of the late Mr. Doughty's suits of solemn black into a trim-fitting pair of breeches with a matching short coat.

But Jammy did not join the household in Stoll's Alley. Mrs. Doughty's small home was already crammed to capacity with her own family, Charlotte and Nick, and Phoebe and the baby.

Application made to the magistrate resulted in permission for Jammy to lodge with a Quaker family, friends of Mrs. Doughty, who lived on Meeting Street.

After two nights of sleeping in Mrs. Doughty's cellar, Jammy was willing to move. The Quaker family agreed to take responsibility for him until he became eligible to apply for the General Birch certificate.

Since, for the time being, Jammy was not allowed to leave

the premises of the family on Meeting Street, Phoebe promised to visit him every day.

❖

"Here's something for you, Phoebe," Nick announced when he returned from work the day after Jammy's move. "This has been waiting at the lawyer's office for me to sign. Guard it well."

Phoebe and Charlotte, both busy with mending, looked up from their work. The long document in Nick's hand bore a bright red seal. Phoebe set down the child's stocking she had been darning and took the paper from him. After scanning it for a minute, she read aloud:

> *Province of South Carolina. To all to whom these Presents shall come to be seen or made known, I Nicholas John Schyler send Greeting. Know ye that I the said Nicholas John Schyler have manumitted, enfranchised and set free, and do by these Presents manumit, enfranchise and set free a certain Negro woman named Phoebe of and from all manner of bondage and Slavery whatsoever. To have and to hold such manumission and freedom unto the said Negro woman for ever. In Witness whereof I have hereunto set my Hand and Seal this twenty-seventh day of February in the year of out Lord one thousand seven hundred and eighty-one.*

Charlotte sat listening. So this was the document that she had asked Captain Braemar to pick up if he could. It had remained in the lawyer's office, waiting for Nick to sign it.

Phoebe looked up. "Thank you, Mr. Nick. All my life I've dreamed of freedom." For a moment she appeared incapable of saying more. Then she added in a low voice. "There's one thing missing. This paper doesn't say anything about Noah."

"Since I didn't own him, it wasn't in my power to manumit him."

"Then he still belongs to Mr. Morley?"

"Legally, he does. But you have nothing to fear from him. Mr. Morley is locked up in the Provost Dungeon. His house and all his property have been confiscated."

"I'm not surprised to hear that," Charlotte said. "It's what the rebels did to us Loyalists, back in the Mohawk Valley. I'm tempted to say, 'It serves him right.' But in truth, two wrongs don't make a right. What will Mrs. Morley and their children do? It seems harsh to throw the family onto the street."

"Mrs. Morley's sister, Mrs. Vesey, is sending a schooner to take them all to Fair Meadow, the Veseys' plantation up the Cooper River. Don't feel too sorry for Mrs. Morley. The British authorities are allowing her to take not only her clothes and jewellery, but also any slaves who choose to stay in her service."

"Do any choose to stay?" asked Charlotte. "I certainly wouldn't choose to remain in slavery."

"It goes against the grain, doesn't it?" said Nick. "But one slave has chosen to remain."

"Who?" asked Phoebe.

"The nursemaid."

"That's Betty." Phoebe nodded. "I understand. She's getting old and wants to be sure of a roof over her head. She's likely afraid she'll starve if she's on her own. But what about the others?"

"They'll all apply for the General Birch certificate. The butler will serve by polishing British officers' boots. The laundress will wash their clothes. The cook will prepare meals for the new residents of Morley's house."

"I already know what Jammy will do," Phoebe exclaimed. "He wants to enlist in Colonel Thompson's cavalry unit, the Independent Troop of Black Dragoons."

"That will be perfect for him," said Charlotte, "with all his experience around horses."

Nick turned to Charlotte. "Sweetheart, I have some news for you, too."

"Yes?"

"Morley's house has been assigned as living quarters for the Civilian Department of Southern Command."

"Your department!"

"Exactly. There are eight bedrooms. You and I can have one, if you like."

For a moment her mind dwelt on what this meant. A house in the finest part of town. Dinners prepared by Lewis Morley's cook. A bedroom of their own. A featherbed instead of two straw mattresses on the front room floor.

It was not easy to say no.

"I can't live there, Nick. I'll always remember how I felt

when I learned that the Sons of Liberty had taken over my family's home: sleeping in our beds, warming themselves at our fireplace. I'd consider myself no better than those villains if I were to do the same."

"I thought so. That's why I did not put down our name."

# Chapter 29

"THEE NEEDS NOT carry laundry any longer," said Mrs. Doughty, "Nick pays a fair rate for thy lodging. Now that Phoebe has a certificate to prove she is free, she can go about town without hindrance as my helper."

"But I like to!" Charlotte protested. "I need to be useful. If I didn't help you, whatever would I do with myself all day?"

Into her mind came a vision of how Mrs. Knightly spent her days in the officers' quarters. Drinking tea. Planning balls. Being fitted for new gowns. No. That was not the life Charlotte wanted.

She would have liked work that was both useful and interesting. Apart from the chance to pick up bits of news as she made her rounds, carrying bundles of laundry was hardly interesting. For the time being, she reckoned that she would settle for useful.

Nick bought a two-wheel handcart for her use. It was a great help, once she learned to navigate around potholes and garbage. In her free time she often took Patience, Charity and Joseph for rides—one at a time, for one child was all the handcart could carry.

On these excursions she saw white labourers and free blacks working together to repair the fortifications. Little more than a year ago, the British bombardment had knocked them down. Now another siege seemed likely. This time it would be rebels attacking the British occupiers.

Tension gripped the city. Only the most optimistic Loyalists clung to the dream that victory was still within their grasp.

Still, despite every rebel victory, gentlemen in coffee houses assured each other, as long as Fort Ninety-Six remained in British hands, everything might still be fine. Fort Ninety-Six. The key to the backcountry: that's what Nick had called it. Captain Braemar was one of its defenders. His regiment had gone there right after he gave Charlotte the news of Nick's capture by ruffians. It was where Elijah would be now, if he had not deserted. Fort Ninety-Six, with its prosperous village, was the stronghold where the loyal forces would make their stand.

It was no wonder that she listened especially for news of

Ninety-Six. In the spring of 1781 its fate hung in the balance. The fortress was under attack. For weeks in June the unbeatable General Greene, the Fighting Quaker, had the fort under siege. Short of water, short of food, short of ammunition, the defending army held on, waiting for reinforcements.

Then the miracle happened. General Greene gave up. One fine day, he abandoned the siege and marched his army away.

For one week, there was great joy in Charleston.

Just one week. Then everything changed.

Charlotte, on her laundry rounds, had never before heard such mutterings of betrayal as she heard when the news arrived that the defenders of Ninety-Six, after driving off General Green's rebel forces, had destroyed their own fort and burned the village to the ground.

Gentlemen milled about in front of the London Coffee House on King Street.

"I can't believe it," one gentleman said, lifting his nose from his copy of the *Royal Gazette*. "The rebels had retreated. Fort Ninety-Six was saved."

"Madness."

"Utter folly."

It made no sense to Charlotte either.

Nick returned late that evening. Charlotte had waited up for him, a lit candle in the front room window, worrying lest he had come to harm. At his approach, she opened the door.

As soon as he entered, he sank wearily onto the settle. She sat down beside him.

"Have you heard about Ninety-Six?" he asked.

"Yes. I don't understand why an army would destroy its own fort."

"I can explain. More than a month ago, Southern Command decided that Ninety-Six was too remote to maintain. It sent orders to Commander Cruger to abandon it. The orders were sent repeatedly. Not one courier got through.

"So Commander Cruger didn't know he was under orders to abandon the fort. His duty, so far as he knew, was to defend it. And that's what he did.

"He had requested reinforcements. When they finally arrived, the rebels had already given up the siege. With the reinforcements came the orders that had failed to arrive weeks before."

"I see," said Charlotte. "So after saving Ninety-Six, his army now had to destroy it." She wondered how Commander Cruger could bear to carry out such orders.

"Yes. He had to command his men to tear down the fortifications and to burn the village. The church. The tavern. The courthouse. The jail. The houses. All went up in flames."

"What will happen to the people who lived in the village?"

"My department has two weeks to get ready for a thousand more refugees."

"Where will you put them?"

"I don't know. Every bit of vacant land is already filled with homeless people. In the camp just outside town, families are living in huts made of scraps of canvas, smashed carts and palmetto leaves. I've seen wagons arriving from the interior with men between the shafts because their horses have been stolen or their oxen eaten. Now worse is to come."

&#10086;

On a hot August afternoon, Charlotte was returning to Stoll's Alley from picking up laundry. The streets were jammed with people pushing wheelbarrows and handcarts. Some had bundles tied on their backs. None looked as if they knew where they were going.

She felt tired and sweaty as she reached Mrs. Doughty's door. Her hand was on the latch when suddenly a half brick shot by her and smashed a pane in the front window. She put her hand up to shield her eyes from the flying shards. Something sharp struck her brow.

Blood was running into her eyes as she opened the door and pushed the handcart inside.

"Thee is hurt!" Mrs. Doughty rushed to her and shut the door. Phoebe jumped up from the braided rug, where she had been playing with the children. At the sight of blood streaming down Charlotte's face, Patience, Charity, Joseph and Noah began to cry. Mrs. Doughty and Phoebe led Charlotte into the kitchen, and helped her to a chair.

"Let me see," said Mrs. Doughty.

"It's nothing." Charlotte struggled to control the shakiness of her voice.

"God be thanked thine eye has been spared." Mrs. Doughty pressed a folded cloth against her brow. "This will staunch the flow of blood."

Charlotte heard another smash as a second windowpane shattered. "Who's doing this? Why?"

"Ruffians. The city is in turmoil. At times like these, people look for somebody to blame for everything. Outsiders make a good target."

The noise in front of the house had stopped.

"Hold this here." Mrs. Doughty pressed Charlotte's fingers to the cloth on her brow. She went into the front room and looked out the window. "Some good citizens have come to our aid. They're holding the ruffians. It's all over."

At least for now, Charlotte thought.

"I'll put sticking plaster on thy cut," said Mrs. Doughty. Calmly she mixed up a thick white paste in a little cup and applied a dab of it to Charlotte's brow. "Rest for a bit while this hardens. Then change thy gown."

Charlotte glanced down. Her skirt and bodice were splattered with blood.

"One of the Friends, a carpenter, will repair the window," said Mrs. Doughty. "I'll write a note for thee to deliver to him when thee is feeling better."

"I can deliver it," said Phoebe.

"No," said Mrs. Doughty. "Thee is safer indoors while there's such unrest."

While Phoebe fetched Charlotte a tumbler of water, Mrs.

Doughty took a quill, an inkhorn and a sheet of paper from her cupboard and, sitting at the kitchen table, began to write. Her hands were red and cracked, and her fingernails split. Washerwoman's hands.

By the time Mrs. Doughty finished writing, the children had stopped crying. After a few more minutes' rest, Charlotte changed her gown.

Mrs. Doughty handed her the note. The name on the front was Levi Blount. The address was on Meeting Street.

"Is that close to Mrs. Perkins' house?" Charlotte asked.

"Two doors further. There's a small community of Friends whose houses are close together."

"I reckon you'd be safer if you dwelt among them."

"Indeed, we would be safer, instead of being the only Friends living in Stoll's Alley." She paused. "Caleb bought this house because the location was convenient for his customers. The front room was his shop."

"Now that things are different, have you thought of moving?"

"That suggestion has been made." Mrs. Doughty picked up her broom and began to sweep together the shards of broken glass.

Charlotte still felt shaky as she left the house, glancing this way and that to be sure no more bricks were coming her way.

In a few minutes she arrived at the plain clapboard house two doors past Mrs. Perkins' home. As she lifted the knocker, she felt very conscious of the patch of sticking plaster on her forehead.

An elderly woman dressed in Quaker black came to the door.

"I have a message for Friend Levi Blount," said Charlotte.

"Levi!" the old woman called to someone in another room.

Charlotte, assuming that she was calling her husband, was surprised to see a man no more than forty years of age come to the door. Under the brim of his black hat, his dark sideburns were barely touched with grey.

He took the message from her and invited her to step inside. Would she like a drink of water? She must be hot after her walk.

"No, thank you. I must get back."

She left him reading the note.

The next morning, Friend Levi arrived at Mrs. Doughty's door, carrying a toolbox. Like all Quakers, he had a sober, serious manner. Mrs. Doughty's manner was equally sober and serious. She enquired after his mother's health and gave him no more than a modest smile.

From his toolbox Friend Levi took a measuring tape and heavy leather gloves. After removing the remaining bits of broken glass, he measured the window opening for new panes.

Before leaving, he said to Mrs. Doughty, "A young woman like thee should be living closer to other Friends, not in

Stoll's Alley, where there is no family that shares our faith."

"I manage very well, Friend Levi. Most of the time."

When he returned, he brought two squares of glass and a small quantity of putty. Setting to work with few words, he finished the job quickly.

Mrs. Doughty thanked him and then added, "Perhaps I'll see thee at meeting tomorrow."

"I'll come by for thee. I don't like the thought of thee walking out alone."

Charlotte noticed that Mrs. Doughty blushed before lowering her face.

# Chapter 30

"THINGS CAN'T GO on like this much longer," said Nick. He was sitting up in the darkness. It was the middle of the night, but he could not sleep. "Charleston's a powder keg ready to blow up. We've jammed the freed slaves who work on fortifications into an old sugar factory, where living conditions are worse than they endured in slavery. They're angry about this. When we offered them freedom, they expected something better. And the backcountry Loyalists who've fled to Charleston are just as badly off."

"What do you fear will happen?" asked Charlotte.

"Riots. Bloodshed. Cholera. On top of everything else, General Greene's army is fifteen miles away, with nothing standing in the way of a siege."

"Do you think he'll attack?"

"He may not need to. Sieges cost lives. I think he'll wait to see what happens in Virginia. General Cornwallis is on his way there to fight George Washington's army. Cornwallis wants to bring on a decisive battle. He thinks he can win. If he does win, he'll finally be able to join forces with General Clinton's army in the north."

Charlotte nodded. "That's if he wins. I reckon if Washington wins, that will be even more decisive."

All through the long, hot summer of 1781, Charleston held its breath and waited for the decisive battle that General Cornwallis was so eager to bring on. At last, at Yorktown in Virginia on October 19th, the battle took place. But Cornwallis did not achieve the result he desired. His surrender was total.

The news arrived the next day. Seven thousand and eighty-seven British and Loyalist officers and men were prisoners of war. Nine hundred British seamen were prisoners of war. One hundred and forty-four cannons were turned over to the rebels, as well as fifteen galleys, a frigate, and thirty transport ships. Cornwallis, pleading illness, did not attend the surrender ceremony but sent his second-in-command.

People gathered in front of the coffee houses and on street corners talking about it. They spoke quietly, soberly. Was this the end of the war?

Again Nick arrived home after everyone had finished eating and the children were in bed. He sank in weariness onto his chair at the kitchen table. Charlotte took from the food locker the biscuit and grits she had saved for him.

"This is the first I've eaten since breakfast," he said between bites. "It's been a hard day."

She sat beside him to keep him company, not speaking much until he was finished, and then she said, "Everybody's talking about the news from Yorktown. They say it's the end of the war."

"It's not," he answered. "General Clinton's army is undefeated in the north, and the rebels lack the strength to take New York.

"I'll tell you some other news I learned today. Ralph Braemar's parents have set sail for Jamaica. They chartered a ship, and off they went. With them they took their money and valuables, as well as a hundred slaves from their rice plantation. Mr. Braemar's name is sure to be on the list of Tories whose property will be confiscated when the rebels win. He saw the wisdom of getting out before he lost everything."

"What about Captain Braemar? Where's he?"

"I suppose Ralph's a prisoner of war in Virginia. After Fort Ninety-Six was abandoned, his regiment was attached to Cornwallis' army. Most likely Ralph will join his parents in Jamaica when the prisoners of war are released."

"Then you're likely never to see him again."

"I suppose not, and that's a pity. He's been a good friend." For a moment Nick's thoughts seemed to be far away. "I'll try to get in touch with him when the war's over and I have more time."

"That should be soon, the way things are going."

"Not soon. We have to wait for Parliament to decide whether it wants to continue the war. Now that France has thrown its support behind the rebels, I think Parliament will vote to quit the struggle and let the Thirteen Colonies go their own way."

"You mean, let them have their own country?"

"That's not such a bad idea. I don't like slavery. I don't like their treatment of the native people. But I've no doubt the Continental Congress is capable of running a country. When Britain stops thinking of these people as colonists and starts thinking of them as trading partners, both sides will be better off. But there's nothing we can do about it. We have to wait and see what Parliament decides."

"Nick! That will take months!"

"I know. First a ship carries the news to England. Then Parliament spends weeks debating the issues. After the vote's finally taken, a ship has to bring the decision to North America."

"I don't like to admit that the rebels are right about anything," said Charlotte. "But being loyal doesn't mean that you want to be ruled by a government on the other side of the Atlantic Ocean."

"Charlotte, that's what I've been saying from the start. And it's something that must happen. Within five years there'll be ten thousand Loyalists settled in the Upper Country and thirty thousand in Nova Scotia. After what these people are going through, they'll surely have earned the right to manage their own affairs."

"Will Britain let them?"

"After losing thirteen colonies, I think Britain will learn a lesson," said Nick. "It may take years to persuade Britain to hand over the reins, but in time it will happen."

# Chapter 31

WAS THERE A WAR going on, or not?

Nathanael Greene's army had its heavy guns pointing at the Charleston Peninsula from both sides, but not a shot was fired. Charlotte suspected that the so-called Fighting Quaker didn't really like fighting, or at least did not like unnecessary bloodshed. Maybe he had not abandoned every principle of his religion. For the present, he seemed content to sit and wait.

But while Charleston remained free from attack, there was plenty of backcountry fighting. Skirmishes and raids continued throughout the months of waiting for the ship that would bring Parliament's decision. Nick reported that the Black Dragoons had been in several minor battles. Phoebe had not seen Jammy for months, but never lost faith that he would be back.

In February 1782, the news arrived from London. It was exactly what Nick had foretold. Parliament responded to Cornwallis' surrender by voting to halt all military operations in the New World. Peace negotiations were underway. The United States of America was about to be born.

At last it's over, Charlotte thought. The news made her neither happy nor sad. On the evening of the day that Parliament's decision arrived, Charlotte would have liked to go for a walk with Nick, but with so many desperate, homeless people everywhere, the streets were unsafe after dark. And so Charlotte and Nick sat in the front room, warmed by a small fire. They held hands but talked little.

Charlotte's heart held more than words could express. She had lost her brothers, her mother, and her home because of the war. This had been the price of loyalty to King George. And it had all been in vain.

Nick also had suffered loss. At the beginning of the war he, like his father, had supported the revolution. But when the violence of the Sons of Liberty caused Nick to change sides, old Mr. Schyler, a Patriot to the core, called him a turncoat and threw him out.

We've both been hurt, Charlotte thought, but the end of the war somehow sets us free. Her fingers tightened around Nick's hand. At odds with her serious mood was a sense of starting out on a new adventure.

She turned to Nick. "Do you think we'll be back on Carleton Island by summer?"

He shook his head.

One evening in March, Nick brought home a copy of the *Royal Gazette* and spread it on the kitchen table for Charlotte and Phoebe to read. Only they and Noah were at home, for Mrs. Doughty had taken her children to a Quaker gathering. Recently, she seemed to spend a lot of time at meetings of the Friends.

"Remember that list of names the rebels were making?" said Nick.

"The list of people who'll be banished and have their property seized?"

"That's right. Here it is. The *Royal Gazette* obtained a copy."

"Six classes of persons," Charlotte read. "Class One: British subjects who never submitted to the American Government. Oh, look! There's a John Braemar near the top of the list. Is that Captain Braemar's father?"

"It is. He escaped with his fortune just in time. Others weren't so lucky."

She read on silently, then exclaimed, "Look at this, Nick. 'Class Five: anyone holding a civil or military position during the British occupation of Charleston.'" She laughed. "That's you. They're going to seize your property."

"They would if I had any."

"Here's Class Six: 'Obnoxious persons.' I wonder what makes a person obnoxious?"

"Owning property that somebody with influence wants to get his hands on."

Charlotte shook her head. "This would be funny if it weren't so mean."

"Four hundred and twenty-five families are on that list. If you hadn't rescued me, there'd be a hundred more, because no one staked out on a hill of fire ants remains silent for long."

Nick folded the newspaper. "There's one more piece of news I must tell you. Lewis Morley's out of prison. He was released today in an exchange of prisoners of war."

Phoebe's head jerked up. "Mr. Morley's free!" She looked anxiously toward the door, as if she expected her former master to come barging through.

"Where is he now?" Charlotte asked Nick.

"He's gone up the Cooper River to Fair Meadow, where his wife and children have been staying with Mrs. Morley's sister. He'll bring his family back to Charleston as soon as his agent has reclaimed his house."

"The house where you and I could have had a room!" Charlotte shrugged. "Easy come, easy go."

"My fellow workers are scrambling about, trying to find places to live, though they won't need them for long. The British Commander at Charleston, General Leslie, is expecting orders to evacuate the city. England will send a fleet to carry all of us away."

"All of us? Everybody?"

"All the British and Loyalist soldiers who happen to be in South Carolina when the fighting ends, as well as more than four thousand white Loyalists and six thousand former slaves."

"So the rebels won't be getting back their slaves," said Charlotte.

"That's right. In the peace negotiations, England refused to back down on that issue. Any holder of a General Birch certificate is excluded from the agreement to return property seized from rebels. But we can't call them rebels any longer. They're Americans."

"Americans. Well, I reckon we'll have to get used to that."

Phoebe spoke up. "What will happen to the Black Dragoons."

"They'll be disbanded and evacuated by ship."

"Even Jammy?"

"Jammy has no choice. When the Americans take over, they'll hang every Black Dragoon they can catch. Not one runaway slave who fought on the British side will be spared."

Phoebe flinched. "Where will the ships take the Black Dragoons?"

"To Nova Scotia."

"What about you and Miss Charlotte?"

"We'll take ship to Nova Scotia, too. But then we'll continue on to the Upper Country, to Carleton Island."

Phoebe bit her lower lip. "I'm going to miss you. You're the best friends I've ever had."

Before she could say more, the front door opened. Patience, Charity and Joseph ran into the house, followed by Mrs. Doughty.

"How was the meeting?" Charlotte asked. "You've been away for two hours. That's a long time for the little ones."

"Not too long," said Mrs. Doughty.

"It was *very* long," Patience insisted. "But afterwards, Friend Levi's mother gave us raisin cake."

"Oh," said Charlotte. "How delicious!"

"I had three pieces," Joseph said, "and then Friend Levi carried me piggyback all the way home."

Mrs. Doughty sat down at the table. Charlotte noticed that her face was flushed.

"We've been talking about the evacuation of Charleston," said Nick. "In the fall, Charlotte and I will take ship for Halifax. So you won't have such a crowd in your home."

Phoebe burst in. "Noah and I will stay . . . if you want us. I can help with laundry and housework. I can mind the little ones while you go to meetings."

"Phoebe, thee and Noah will have a home with me as long as thee wishes. But it will not be here in Stoll's Alley."

"Mrs. Doughty," said Charlotte, "what do you mean? Have you decided to move to Meeting Street to live among the Friends?"

Under the deep brim of her bonnet, Mrs. Doughty's cheeks turned redder than ever. Charlotte guessed what she was about to say before the words left her mouth.

"Friend Levi has asked me to be his wife."

# Chapter 32

AFTER THAT DAY, Mrs. Doughty never worked as a washer-woman again.

The wedding would not take place until after Charlotte and Nick had left for Nova Scotia. That time was clearly coming soon. In July the British fleet evacuated Savannah. On August 12, 1782, the *Royal Gazette* announced that Charleston would be next.

It happened in October. Phoebe and Charlotte were cooking supper when Nick strolled into the kitchen.

"We leave tonight," he said, and he patted the leather pouch he wore on his belt. "My orders are here."

Charlotte looked up from the pile of oysters she and Phoebe were shucking.

"Tonight!"

So the time had come at last. The excitement that had been building up in her under a pretence of calm suddenly flared into panic.

"Nick, I can't get ready that fast!"

"Yes, you can. It won't take half an hour to throw your clothes into your trunk. After supper, when we're packed, a carter will carry our trunks to the wharf. A fleet of forty ships is waiting in the harbour."

"It's been waiting there for days. Why the hurry now?"

"The fleet's been waiting to catch the wind. For days it's been blowing from the east. Now it's switching to the west. We set sail on the morning tide."

"You'd better get started," said Phoebe. "I'll finish making supper. It will be ready by the time Mrs. Doughty returns home."

Charlotte set down her oyster knife. When she looked up, she saw a smile on Nick's face.

"And here's some good news. When we get to Carleton Island, I'll be working at Fort Haldimand, where you and I shall have a room in the officers' quarters. It's all settled."

She laughed. "As I recall, it was all settled for us to live in the officers' quarters here in Charleston."

"No fear this time. My work's cut out for me. No more carrying messages. No more spy missions. There are more than five hundred Loyalists to be evacuated from Carleton Island. My assignment is help organize their move to the mainland."

"But why do they have to leave Carleton Island?"

"They have to leave because Carleton Island will be part of the United States of America. According to the treaty of peace, the international border will run between Carleton Island and Wolfe Island.

"The British government has bought a huge tract of land from the Mississaugas. It covers Cataraqui, the Bay of Quinte, and the north shore of the St. Lawrence River. This area is where Loyalists will receive their land grants. That includes you and me, dearest. As soon as we reach the Upper Country, I can register our names. Before long, you and I will own land of our own."

"Nick, that's marvellous. I can hardly wait!"

"When you're gone, will you write to me, Miss Charlotte?" Phoebe asked.

"Of course. And you must write to me. I'll write down directions for you to address your letters."

Suddenly there was a knock at the door. A knock so loud it made Charlotte jump.

"Who might that be?" she exclaimed.

The caller knocked again.

She hurried into the front room and opened the door.

A carriage drawn by a roan horse stood waiting in the street. On the doorstep stood a well-dressed gentleman whom she had never seen before. He wore a tricorn hat, a dark blue velvet frockcoat, and a ruffled shirt of dazzling white muslin. Grey eyes stared boldly from a cruel but handsome face.

Grey eyes. Like Noah's. A chill ran down Charlotte's spine.

"I believe this is the Widow Doughty's house?" He had the easy manner of a man of the world.

"It is."

"And a black girl named Phoebe is living here?"

"Yes."

"Please fetch her." He stepped into the room without invitation, as if sure of his right to enter any habitation that he chose.

"Phoebe is not to be fetched," Charlotte bristled. "I'm sure she hears your voice. She will come if she chooses."

Turning her head, she saw that Phoebe was already entering the room. She held Noah by the hand, his grey eyes peeking from around her skirt. Nick stood in the kitchen doorway, watching.

"Well, Phoebe," the man said. "I hear that you're a free woman now."

"Yes, sir. I am free." Phoebe's manner showed that same dignity Charlotte had noticed at the slave market.

"But your child is not." He spoke with the confidence of someone accustomed to having his own way. "The fact is, Phoebe, you're in possession of stolen property."

Phoebe held her ground. "I'm free. My son is free."

"Now, Phoebe, you know better than that. You were my property at the time of his birth. That makes him my property." There was not so much as a glimmer of kindness in his grey eyes. Only steely determination.

Charlotte spoke up. "This little boy is free. He has lived for a year behind British lines."

"That's right," Nick added. "He's entitled to a General Birch certificate."

Morley laughed. "Those rules no longer apply. Remember, the British lost the war. They aren't handing out any more General Birch certificates. I've already looked into this. If a runaway slave already holds a valid certificate, the United States of America will recognize his freedom. Wisely or not, the terms of peace make that provision. But I doubt that this child . . ." At that moment he really looked at Noah for the first time. When he saw the eyes that were the colour of his own, he flinched.

It took a moment for him to recover his self-possession. Then he continued. "I doubt whether a child this young has assisted the British for the required year."

Phoebe's voice was fierce. "You can't have him."

"Mr. Morley, you must leave," said Charlotte. "If Mrs. Doughty were here, she would not welcome you under her roof."

"Then let's take care of this business before she returns. I have a buyer for the boy, a wealthy planter whose son is one year old. He wishes to purchase a suitable boy to be a lifetime servant for his son. He wants one who's about the same age, so they can grow up together."

"Get out!" Nick strode to the door, raising one closed fist. He looked as if he could, and would, hurl Morley into the street.

Morley protested. "Sir, it is none of your business what I do with this child. I have suffered a good deal at the hands of the Tories. I was imprisoned in a dungeon. My warehouse was seized. My house was occupied by pen pushers who drank all my wine. It will take months to rebuild my business. Some reparation is due. If I can make a few pounds by selling a piece of my property, that surely is my right."

"A human being is not property." Nick's voice was cold with contempt.

Morley blustered. "I had hoped to handle this with no fuss. Since that isn't possible, I'll be back tomorrow with a magistrate's order and a couple of strong men to back it up." He glared at Phoebe. "Punishment will be severe if you attempt to hide the child." His lips compressed into an ugly line.

As he turned to leave, he bumped right into Mrs. Doughty coming through the doorway, followed by Patience, Charity and Joseph.

"Excuse me," he said, and kept on going.

For a long moment no one spoke. Mrs. Doughty broke the silence. "What was Mr. Morley doing here?"

"He's going to take my baby and sell him. Mrs. Doughty,

please help me!" Dropping to her knees beside Noah, she wrapped her arms around her child and buried her face in his soft neck.

Charlotte and Nick explained to Mrs. Doughty all that had happened.

When they finished, Mrs. Doughty said, "I'm not sure what we can do. But one thing is certain: Phoebe and Noah must leave Charleston before morning."

# Chapter 33

"WE MUST TAKE them with us to Nova Scotia," said Charlotte.

"They can't come with us," said Nick. "Phoebe didn't enroll. Her name isn't on the passenger list."

"There must be a way."

"Earlier, I might have been able to do something. But it's too late. Enrollment closed in mid-August."

"But surely, no one would object."

Nick shook his head. "There won't be any exceptions, not even on compassionate grounds. The Savannah evacuation was a madhouse, with Loyalists battling each other to get onto the boats that would carry them out to the ships.

Southern Command is determined not to let that happen here. This time, rules will be strictly enforced." His voice fell. "I'm sorry. It's beyond my control."

"Will thee stand by while this child is taken from his mother and sold?" Mrs. Doughty's determined blue eyes regarded Nick steadily. "What good are thy principles if thee fails to act upon them?"

Phoebe was crying and Noah was crying. Patience and Charity did the most sensible thing and took Joseph outside for a ride in the handcart.

Charlotte waited a moment for Nick to say something. When he did not, she said hesitatingly, "What if . . . ?"

He turned his head toward her. "Yes?"

"What if . . . we smuggle them on board?" Charlotte pointed to her trunk. "If I take out half my clothes and if Phoebe bends her knees, she'll fit."

"You and I have been given a cabin," Nick said thoughtfully. "If the trunk is brought to our cabin and not loaded into the hold . . . Yes. That will work."

Mrs. Doughty regarded the trunk. "I can ask Friend Levi to bring his brace and bit to bore air holes."

Phoebe lifted her face. "You can put me in that trunk, but not Noah."

"Of course not," Charlotte assured her. "He'd cry. Even with you holding him, he'd be terrified."

"Then how can you get him onto the ship?" Phoebe asked.

"In my arms. Look at him and look at me. My hair is black and nearly as curly. His skin is not much darker than mine. Who's to say he's not mine if I take him aboard?"

"He hasn't been enrolled, either," Mrs. Doughty pointed out.

"For a baby, that's less of a problem," said Nick. "We've been working on the evacuation for months. Since we started enrolling passengers, dozens of women have given birth. Nobody's going to check the passenger list for a babe in arms."

Mrs. Doughty looked skeptical. "Noah's not a babe in arms. He's twenty-two months old."

"Look at Charlotte. A big strapping girl is bound to have a big strapping baby."

If the situation were not so serious, Charlotte might have hit him. Instead, she threw back her head and laughed.

That broke the tension. Everybody laughed.

"We'll wrap Noah in a blanket and I'll carry him," said Charlotte. "Maybe no one will notice he's the wrong size."

"What about me?" Phoebe asked. "You can't keep me in a trunk all the way to Nova Scotia."

"We'll figure it out as we go along," said Nick. "If you're discovered after we're underway, the ship won't turn back. Phoebe, nobody's going to throw you overboard. I may find myself in a bit of trouble, but I'll take that as it comes. We just have to smuggle you aboard and keep you hidden until we're at sea."

"But what will happen to me and Noah when we get to Nova Scotia?"

"The harbour's at a town called Halifax," said Nick. "Charlotte and I will find you and Noah a place to stay."

Phoebe lowered her face. "I won't know anybody there."

"Don't worry," said Charlotte. "We'll see that you're comfortably settled before we go on to the Upper Country."

"You won't be lonely," said Nick. "Hundreds of holders of General Birch certificates will be evacuated from Charleston to Halifax. You're almost certain to find people you know. And you'll make new friends."

"Jammy will never be able to find me."

"Yes, he will!" Charlotte exclaimed. "When my family fled from the Mohawk Valley, nobody knew where we were going. Not even Nick. But he found me. Knowing Jammy, I'm sure he can track you down."

"It may be a year before the Black Dragoons are evacuated," said Nick. "So you must be patient. When Jammy's ship reaches Halifax, he'll find you."

Nick turned to Mrs. Doughty. "What's Friend Levi's address? I'll go now to ask him to bring his brace and bit."

"His horse and cart, too," said Mrs. Doughty. "So he can carry the trunks to the wharf."

Everything was done in such a rush that there was little time for embraces and goodbyes. Levi Blount drilled the holes in Charlotte's trunk and helped Nick load the trunks onto his cart. There was just enough room on the narrow seat for Charlotte to sit beside Friend Levi, with Noah on her lap. Nick walked behind.

Noah seemed happy to be riding on the cart, pulled by Friend Levi's bay mare. His mother being in the trunk did not disturb him. He had watched her step into it and lie down on top of Charlotte's old blue gown.

"It's a game like peek-a-boo," Phoebe had explained. "You won't see me before we're on the big boat. And then I'll pop up to surprise you."

By the time they reached the harbour, Noah was asleep.

Their ship was the *Esperanza*, tied up at Wharf Eight and ready to board.

"It's bigger than the *Blossom*," Charlotte said to Nick, "and looks much cleaner."

"She's a new ship, built to carry spices and passengers in the West Indies trade. Britain requisitioned her for evacuating troops and Loyalists. She's already served in the evacuation of Savannah. In due time, she'll transport Loyalists and troops from New York City."

"There's even a gangway, so we don't have to climb a ladder. I was wondering how I'd do that, carrying Noah."

"Come." Nick helped her down from the cart and tucked a blanket around Noah. "Let's go aboard."

A young officer stood at the top of the gangway, holding an open register in his hands. His polished buttons gleamed in the moonlight. He waved to Nick, who waved back. Then Nick and Friend Levi carried first Nick's trunk and then

Charlotte's onto the deck. Charlotte followed.

They thanked Friend Levi and said goodbye, wishing him happiness as a married man.

Under the brim of his black hat, there was a twinkle in his eye. "I have found me a fine wife, and three children ready-made. Who could ask the Lord for a greater blessing?" With that, he took his leave.

"Glad to see you, Nick," said the young officer.

"Glad to be aboard, Harry. Is your regiment stopping in Halifax or going on to Montreal?"

"Don't know yet. Waiting for orders. What about you?"

"I've been assigned to Carleton Island to help move Loyalists to the mainland."

Charlotte, trying to be inconspicuous, moved into the shadow of a large crate. Her trunk and Nick's lay on the deck beside her. She hoped Nick and his friend wouldn't talk too long, because Noah was getting heavier every second.

"I need these trunks in our cabin," Nick was saying. "There are papers in them I have to work on during the voyage. I can't take any chance these trunks will end up in the hold."

Glancing toward the trunks, the officer noticed Charlotte.

"I've not been introduced to Mrs. Schyler."

"Oh." Nick beckoned her to approach. "Charlotte, I'd like you to meet Captain Moss. Harry, may I present my wife Charlotte."

She bowed as well as she could while holding a twenty-pound toddler in her arms.

"Honoured to make your acquaintance, Mrs. Schyler." He

turned to Nick. "You never mentioned you and your wife had a baby."

"Didn't I? It must have slipped my mind."

"That's just like you!" Captain Moss laughed. "Always with your nose in a book or your head in the clouds. You never notice what's happening in the real world."

"About those trunks . . ." Nick said.

Captain Moss called to two soldiers who stood at the railing. Taking a quick look at the sheet of paper in his hand, he said. "Men, take these trunks to Cabin 10."

"It's not busy now," he said to Nick. "Most passengers are already aboard."

The west wind carried the sound of St. Michael's bells to Charlotte's ears. She stood listening, knowing that she would never again hear their beautiful music upon the night air. Then she and Nick went below.

Phoebe sat up groggily, one hand pressing the top of her head.

"How was it?" Charlotte asked.

"Just fine, until we went on board. After that, whoever was carrying the trunk didn't know they had a passenger inside. They were shifting me this way and that, and then they tipped me headfirst." She rubbed the top of her head. "I got a bit of a bump."

"That must have been while they were taking the trunk down to the cabin."

"I didn't know what was going on. But as long as I could hear people talking, I wasn't afraid."

Nick kindled a whale oil lamp that was bolted to a little table which in turn was bolted to the floor.

By its light Charlotte saw that the cabin was small and neat. Two bunks, two chairs, and one table. There was a window with four tiny panes.

"I like this ship." Charlotte sniffed. "It smells of spices. Cinnamon. Nutmeg. Ginger."

Noah was already asleep on the lower bunk, where Charlotte had laid him down. He had not wakened since dozing off in Friend Levi's cart. Phoebe crawled into the bunk beside him.

"We all need some rest," said Nick.

Charlotte scrambled up the ladder to the top bunk, followed by Nick.

"This is so much nicer than the *Blossom*," she said, snuggling against him. As she listened to the lapping of water against the hull, she felt a peace like a blanket drawn about them. Soon the gentle rocking of the ship lulled them both to sleep.

When she woke in the morning, a low sun was streaming through the little window of the cabin. Footsteps thumped on the deck planks overhead. She felt the ship surging forward.

"Wake up!" she nudged Nick. "We're moving. Let's go on deck!"

"You must go alone," he grunted. "If we're both on deck at the same time, we have to take Noah with us, and he's still sleeping."

"Phoebe's here."

"Nobody but us knows that. You and I came aboard with a baby. What sort of parents would leave a baby alone in a cabin while they went up on deck?"

She hadn't thought about that. But now she did. "Nick, I'm afraid this is going to be a complicated voyage."

"For the past four years, my life has been a complicated voyage. Bringing an illegal passenger on board is just one more complication."

She kissed him. "Go back to sleep, dearest. Everything's going to be fine." She scrambled down the ladder from the bunk.

As she left the cabin and made her way to the steep stairs that led up to the deck, Charlotte was not sorry to be alone. Her mind was filled with hopes and fears. She needed to be by herself to think.

Not that she was alone when she reached the deck. Other passengers were clustered in little knots. Men and women. Families. Black people talking with other blacks, white people with other whites. Still separated, although bound together in their fate.

These were the Loyalists of the Carolinas. She heard their soft southern accents, as well as the unfamiliar sounds of the Gullah tongue spoken by some of the former slaves. Their sad voices mingled with the creaking of masts and spars as the *Esperanza*, carried by the tide and driven by an offshore wind, crossed the harbour bar.

Gladness filled her heart at the thought of returning to the Upper Country. But no signs of joy brightened the faces of her fellow passengers. They were leaving forever the land of their birth. Their hearts were in the Carolinas. All that awaited them in the unknown country to the north were forests to be cleared, homes to be built, and the certainty of hardship for the rest of their lives.

Charlotte felt queasy. It wasn't seasickness, although she intended for a time to pretend it was. She didn't want to alarm Nick, who would probably treat her like an invalid and make her lie down half the day. Already she was aware every minute of the new life she held within her. Before this voyage ended, she would share her news with Nick. Together they would choose a name for a girl, a name for a boy.

# AUTHOR'S NOTE

The wording of the Deed of Manumission setting Phoebe free is adapted from a 1798 Deed of Manumission displayed in the Charleston Museum, Charleston, South Carolina. It reads as follows:

## State of South Carolina

To all to whom these Presents shall come to be seen or made known, I Christopher Rogers of Charleston in the State aforesaid send Greeting. Know ye that I the said Christopher Rogers for and in consideration of the sum of one hundred Pounds Sterling to me in hand well and truly paid at or before the Sealing and Delivery of these Presents and for divers other good causes and considerations me thereunto especially moving, have manumitted, enfranchised and set free, and do by these Presents manumit, enfranchise and set free a certain mulatto man named Jehu Jones of and from all manner of bondage and Slavery whatsoever. To have and to hold such manumission and freedom unto the said Mulatto Man Jehu Jones for ever.

In Witness whereof I have hereunto set my Hand and Seal the twenty second day of January in the year of our Lord one thousand seven hundred and ninety-eight.

# ACKNOWLEDGEMENTS

My thanks to Tony Youmans, Director, Old Exchange Building, Charleston, South Carolina, and to Jennifer Scheetz, Archivist with the Charleston Museum, for giving generously of their time to answer my questions and to direct me to other research sources that I would not have discovered without their help; to Frank Rupert UE, descendant of Loyalists who lived through the siege of Fort Ninety-Six and the subsequent flight to Charleston (and who offered me the loan of his extensive personal library on this subject); to my son John Baxter and his wife Anne Haberl for their patience and good humour in sacrificing their vacation in order to push my wheelchair over the brick sidewalks and cobbled street of Old Charleston after an unlucky accident came close to scuppering my research plans; and to my grandson Thomas Baxter for technical assistance. My thanks also to my daughter Alison Baxter Lean for her invaluable criticism; to my friends Susan Evans Shaw, Barbara Ledger, Trudi Down, Alexandra Gall, Linda Helson and Debbie Welland of the Creative Writing Group, University Women's Club (Hamilton Branch), for their helpful critique of the opening chapters. And finally to Ronald B. Hatch, my publisher, for wanting this book and for always finding a way to be both exacting and encouraging as it developed through various drafts, and to Erinna Gilkison for her insightful editorial comments and practical suggestions.

# ABOUT THE AUTHOR

I have always been a storyteller. When I was about six years old, my mother would set me in a big comfortable chair with my younger brother to entertain him with stories, which I made up as I went along. My ambition as a teenager was to become a journalist. My hometown newspaper, the *Hamilton Spectator*, paid me on a freelance basis for my stories. This was more to my liking than babysitting, and it paid about the same. On enrolling in "English Language and Literature" at the University of Toronto, I still thought of myself as a future journalist. But love of literature got the better of me, and eventually I became a high school English teacher. Always interested in history, I saw a need for young adult novels that would present the story of our country from a Canadian point of view. I wrote *The Way Lies North*, followed by *Broken Trail*, in the hope of helping to meet this need. *Freedom Bound* completes the trilogy dealing with Charlotte and other Loyalist young people, some white, some black and some native, during the American Revolution.

If you would like to contact me, my email address is jeanraebaxter@sympatico.ca. I'll be happy to answer any questions you may have. My website is www.jeanraebaxter.ca. My Facebook page is http://www.facebook.com/JeanRaeBaxterBooks.